Revenge

Though confined by prison walls, King Crawley was a powerful man. Still able to call the shots. Still able to give worse than he got.

Revenge was justice. An eye for an eye, a tooth for a tooth—and a mind for a mind. He plotted a unique kind of murder in which death would come long before the body gasped its last breath. One in which killer and victim would be one and the same.

Sydney Raferty was his target—and through her, he would make her father pay. His weapon was undetectable, untraceable, because it didn't belong in any arsenal. Nevertheless, it was capable of total annihilation....

King Crawley's weapon was love.

Sydney Raferty was King Crawley's first victim. There were two others on his list: Dakota Raferty and Asia Raferty. Their stories are next in Intrigue #163 Squaring Accounts *(June 1991) and #165* No Holds Barred. *(July 1991).*

For Crawley, revenge is sweet....

Dear Reader,

The idea of writing a series of connected mysteries has intrigued me for years. My opportunity and greatest writing challenge came with the idea for "Quid Pro Quo." While the books are interconnected, each story not only stands on its own, but is different from the others in setting and style. You'll go from the Oregon coast to the Olympic Peninsula, from psychological suspense to action adventure. During your travels, I hope you'll enjoy sharing danger and romance with Benno and Sydney, Dakota and Honor, and Dominic and Asia as much as I did while creating their stories.

Follow King Crawley's quest for revenge next month in Intrigue #163, *Squaring Accounts* and in July with Intrigue #165, *No Holds Barred*.

—Patricia Rosemoor

Pushed to
the Limit

Patricia Rosemoor

Harlequin Books

TORONTO • NEW YORK • LONDON
AMSTERDAM • PARIS • SYDNEY • HAMBURG
STOCKHOLM • ATHENS • TOKYO • MILAN

In memory of Jan Milella—
also known as Jan Michaels and Jan Mathews—
a good friend and a better writer.
You are missed.

Harlequin Intrigue edition published May 1991

ISBN 0-373-22161-4

PUSHED TO THE LIMIT

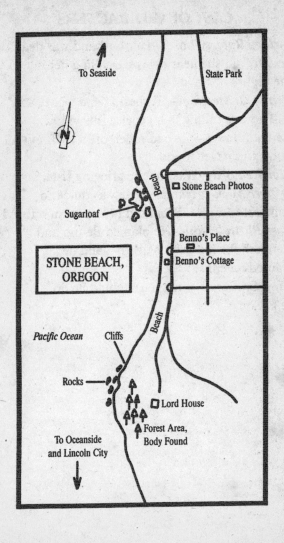

To Seaside

State Park

N

Beach

Stone Beach Photos

Sugarloaf

Benno's Place

Benno's Cottage

STONE BEACH,
OREGON

Pacific Ocean

Cliffs

Beach

Rocks

Lord House

Forest Area,
Body Found

To Oceanside
and Lincoln City

CAST OF CHARACTERS

Sydney Raferty Lord—Her husband was dead. So why did she hear his voice calling her in the night?

Benno DeMartino—His best friend was dead, and he was falling in love with the widow.

Kenneth Lord—He had fallen off a cliff, but his body was never found.

Martha Lord—Was she the grieving sister?

Officer Mick Brickman—He was quick to comfort Martha . What did he expect in return?

Parnell Anderson—He blamed Benno and Kenneth for his sister's death—and he wanted revenge.

King Crawley—What harm could he do in prison?

Prologue

Small and dank, the room vibrated with tension. Suppressing any visible anxiety, he stubbed out his cigarette and clasped his hands into a fist that he rested on the scarred tabletop.

"What did you get on her?" he softly demanded of Lester Freidman.

The accountant threw a quick, nervous look over his shoulder. The guard covering the door nodded and turned his back to them. Lester Freidman slipped his briefcase onto the table, unsnapped the locks and extracted the report from within. He held out the bound sheaf of papers to his employer.

The folder was opened; a photocopy of a newspaper clipping lay on top. Two women posed together.

The less glamorous woman—she was the one. A fringe of bangs framed her large pale eyes, which made her appear a bit fey. The face was rounded, the nose snub. Her build was slight. Unimposing; that's what she was. Nothing extraordinary about her, especially not when compared with her dazzling companion.

"This is going to be almost too easy." He began paging through the report.

"You sure you want to go through with this?" Freidman asked warily.

Movement stopped and eyes filled with rancor made the henchman squirm. "That's a damn stupid question. I've waited too long as it is. Besides, what have I got to lose?"

His laugh echoed through the room. Startled, the guard's head whipped around and made Freidman go pale.

For a brief moment, Freidman's employer tightened his grip on the report. No one on his payroll would dare pity Sydney Raferty.

No one!

Chapter One

Sydney Raferty Lord scrambled along the damp edge of the cliff with her husband of several hours, taking care neither to slip nor to let her camera sway against the rocks. The sky was filled with threatening gray clouds. The gusty wind whipped her heavy skirt around her legs, every so often exposing them to the chill of the moody late-summer day. Far below their treacherous walkway, waves crashed against the Oregon shore, pounded the boulders strewn along the shallows and gouged out crevices that undercut the cliff.

"How about here?" Sydney asked, thinking the spot perfect for a picture.

Kenneth whirled around and, tossing away his cigarette, lifted her into his arms as easily as he'd swept her off her feet when they'd met two weeks earlier. His pale yellow shirt lay half-open. She touched his smooth, tanned chest, and found his warmth reassuring. Kenneth was hers, all solid male, not some metaphysical figment of her imagination as she'd feared so many times over the past few days when reality had blurred with dream.

"You want to do it here?" he asked provocatively, cradling her buttocks and pulling her tightly against him.

His closeness took Sydney's breath away. "I was suggesting taking your picture, you sex maniac."

Dark eyebrows lifted over his heartstopping green eyes and his sculpted features drew into a mock-frown. "Oh. And here I thought you wanted my body, Mrs. Lord."

"I do, Mr. Lord," she assured him, her heart pounding strongly at the notion. She still couldn't get over how much he wanted her. "Maybe we should wait until we get inside your house."

After the justice of the peace had pronounced them man and wife that morning they had headed north for Kenneth's seaside home in Stone Beach. So far, all she'd seen was the outside of the wood structure where they'd left the car.

"I guess I can wait . . . this time," Kenneth finally agreed when a fine spray shot straight up the cliff and misted them.

Sydney felt strangely bereft when her new husband released her. "So, how about that picture?"

"I know the perfect place. It's just ahead. You go up there." He pointed to a spot higher up where saplings bent under the onslaught of ferocious and incessant winds. "You'll get an incredible view of the area . . . and me, of course."

"That's the important part." She stood on tiptoe to brush his lips with hers.

"Mmm, don't tempt me or you'll never get that photo."

Sydney was tempted to forget about her camera altogether, but she wanted to take pictures since these would be the only ones she'd have of her wedding day. With a sigh, she moved away from her husband and the dangerous waters that had played a central part in the disturbing dreams she'd recently had. After a decade of peace the dreams had returned, leaving her anxious and uncertain. She didn't want to be different again. Carefully, she picked her way over rocks and across narrow crevices that would widen with time.

Time. Something she and Kenneth hadn't much of. Being an impulsive person had made her a creative success in advertising, and had prompted her to marry a man she barely knew. But, in work, when things clicked, they clicked. Why should relationships be any different?

They'd met at a beach town farther down the coast where Kenneth had been going over blueprints with a client . . . and where she'd been trying to recuperate— a victim of job burnout. In a search for sanity, Sydney had just quit her job in an L.A. ad agency. She felt she'd made an auspicious start by meeting Kenneth and falling in love with him.

Reaching a flat spot between the windswept trees, she tried to avoid the mud. Kenneth was staring out to sea. Sydney aimed her camera and framed him in the viewfinder, admiring this perfect specimen of the opposite sex. She never judged a man by his looks alone, but it was difficult not to appreciate such male beauty.

Feeling a little silly, Sydney grinned and yelled, "Hey, Mr. Lord!" When he glanced up over his shoulder, she snapped a picture and the film automatically advanced. "Come on, turn around and pose for me!"

Sydney had never thought that she would experience the overwhelming emotions that she felt with Kenneth. After months of being harried, exhausted, more than slightly out of focus, she was overjoyed by these positive feelings.

She was still looking through the camera's lens as her husband turned and waved, then struck a silly pose and gave her the crooked smile that made her heart leap. She was shooting and laughing when his face contorted into a mask of surprise. His arms shot out and he struggled to keep his balance. His upper body wavered and his feet did a bizarre and spasmodic dance.

"Kenneth!"

Frozen and helpless, heart pounding, she watched as if the horror were happening in slow motion. His feet seemed to fly right out from under him. For a second, he was suspended in midair. Then he went down hard and his lower body shot out over the cliff. His mouth opened in a silent scream.

"Kenneth!" Sydney dropped her camera and ran.

Chest flat against rock, he clawed at the smooth surface. Then, with a single shout of defeat, he slid inch by inch and disappeared from sight.

"Oh, my God!" Sydney ran toward the spot where he'd stood only moments ago. "Please, tell me you're all right!"

Her only answer was the crash of ocean against cliff.

Her toe caught the edge of a crevice. Sydney flew forward and fell to her knees. Sobbing now, heedless of her scraped legs, she pushed off from the hard surface and scrambled to her feet. She called to her husband over and over. Nearing the edge of the cliff, she slowed, dropped to her hands and knees and peered over.

"Ken-n-n-eth!"

Voice absorbed by the pounding surf, she scanned the rocks below but could see nothing of Kenneth. He had to be there. She had to get to him . . . help him before . . .

She refused to complete the thought. Instead, terrified, she ran back the way they had come and found a path down to the water's edge. Keeping her footing was impossible. She slipped and slid and clung ferociously to algae-slick rock, all the while scanning the dangerous shallows that drew ever closer.

Nothing.

This didn't make any sense. Kenneth had to be here somewhere. As a wave hit a nearby rock and spewed pebbles at her, Sydney flinched from the pain, turned her head, but continued on. The going was treacherous.

As were her thoughts. What if Kenneth had drowned?

She swallowed the desolate feeling even as she remembered the dream. Boulders had threatened to break *her* body, waves to drown *her*. Not *Kenneth*. But then her dreams were never clear. Her refusal to believe her husband was dead pushed her on, kept her clinging to sharp rocks and continuing to search until her eyes lit on something moving in the water. Kenneth's shirt. She'd found him!

"Hang on!" she gasped, lunging forward.

She touched the cloth, but it slithered through her fingers. She grabbed and yanked. The material pulled free from the tooth of a jagged rock where it had caught. Staring at it, Sydney was swept off her feet by a wave that hit her full-face. A glancing blow stunned her and she swallowed water. She went under. Gagging from the salty taste, sputtering for air, she found a handhold, righted herself and grabbed on to another rock.

Sydney's eyes swept the area in front of her just as the yellow cloth was sucked under the surface by the current.

Just as Kenneth must have been.

Kenneth!

His name echoed in her mind as did the truth she so desperately wanted to deny. Sydney made an unintelligible sound, a mourning for what might have been.

"AND SO, WITH RESPECT, we consign Kenneth Lord's soul to God," Reverend Jonas Taylor said, therewith ending the memorial service.

Calmly, Sydney removed the wedding ring she'd worn for little more than two days. Hardly aware of either the drizzle or the people surrounding her, she ran her fingertip around the thick band, its rough exterior simulating a gold nugget, the inside of it engraved, Kenneth loves Sydney. Silent tears mingled with the light rain to wash her cheeks as she kissed the symbol of a union that hadn't been ordained to endure.

She flung the bit of gold out to sea. Its trajectory was fierce and sure as it joined the man who put it on her finger.

When the ocean roared its acceptance of the token of her love, Sydney closed her eyes. She saw him. Her Kenneth. As alive as he'd been when she'd married him. He stood in the bedroom they would have shared in his house—a house she'd never entered until after he'd died. A vision rather than a memory!

And so real. Oh, so very real. Her head grew light and she swayed as a weak protest passed her lips. A protective arm settled around her shoulders. She opened her eyes. Judge Jasper Raferty was at her side as he always had been whenever one of his children needed him.

"Dad, he can't be dead," she whispered.

Her blood pulsed in jagged throbs and filled her with a mounting anxiety that was all too familiar—an anxiety that had threatened her reason during the past few months. Forehead furrowed, she met her father's expression of concern and pity.

"Now, Sydney, just because the body wasn't found, don't—"

"Dad, please." She would remain calm, but she had to make him understand. "I saw him."

"Where?"

She sensed her father's disbelief before he uttered the question. But then, his doubt didn't surprise her. He'd always been the voice of reason, had always dismissed what he had called her childhood daydreams. He'd never wanted to understand. But she couldn't ignore the light-headed feeling that continued to plague her. Nor the familiar chill. Like a somnambulist, she pulled free of his arms and approached the edge of the cliff.

"Sydney!"

Her sister's worried voice. But Asia was as powerless as their father to stop her.

Sydney dropped to her hands and knees and willed herself to see Kenneth in the water. But, no matter how hard she tried, she couldn't make the image appear.

Instead, she saw the shadowy bedroom and Kenneth holding out his hand for her to join him. Double doors behind Kenneth were open. Wind ruffled his dark hair as it had when he'd been on the cliff. And he was wearing a yellow shirt partially open, revealing his broad chest.

She shivered.

The vision was so real that she fought for a second when strong hands hooked under her arms and lifted. Kenneth's image faded once more, leaving in his place the roiling waters that had left her a widow.

Or had they?

Bewildered, she looked up into her brother's aquamarine eyes shadowed with compassion. Dakota's thick lashes were spiked, wet from the rain that matted his dark ash-blond hair and rolled down his face.

"Come on, Sydney, let's go back to the house," he urged.

"What if Kenneth didn't really drown, Dakota? What if he's not dead?"

"I know you want to believe that—"

"But you don't."

Her brother's eyes mirrored her own perplexity. Of her two siblings, he had always been the one who understood her best. He alone had believed in her ability to see things others couldn't. But even he had been glad when she'd closed off that part of her life and had put it behind her. He'd never said so, but she'd sensed that what others had called her "gift" had made Dakota nearly as uncomfortable as Asia or their parents.

Maybe there was no gift, never had been.

Maybe she *was* going crazy.

"She's just experiencing denial," Asia whispered to their father who stood rigid and white-faced.

"It's natural under the circumstances," Reverend Taylor added.

Yes, natural, Sydney silently echoed. The past few months had been stressful enough to push anyone to the limit. Now this. She was seeing things because she was tired. All she needed was some rest that was undisturbed by dreams. Then she would be fine. She needed to forget about the premonition and get some sleep.

Forget about Kenneth.

Forget....

Staring at the ocean, she told herself she had to make peace with the truth. She must believe her husband had been consigned to a watery grave, his body forever enveloped in cold unfeeling arms. Dead. Kenneth was dead. And so was the fantasy.

She whispered, "Dakota, take me away from here."

He tightened his hold and turned her away from the scene of the nightmarish accident. He started to lead her toward the house that would be hers, at least until Kenneth's estate was settled. Kenneth's parents were long dead and no one had been able to contact his sister Martha in Portland. Sydney couldn't just pack her bags and leave.

"My deepest sympathies, Mrs. Lord," Reverend Taylor said.

"Thank you for coming on such short notice."

"God rarely gives advance warning when he calls his children."

She'd had warning of a sort, Sydney thought guiltily as Dakota urged her forward past the few mourners, but she hadn't known how to interpret the dreams.

How sad that Kenneth's memorial service had only been attended by her own family, the local minister and a couple of residents of the town. Officer Mick Brickman had responded to her call about Kenneth. And the other gentleman present, Parnell Anderson, must have been one of Kenneth's friends. Passing the two men who stood shoulder to shoulder as if they had been sharing secrets, Sydney glanced at Anderson's rough features, which were set in a bland expression hardly indicative of grief.

She must be imagining things again. Why else would the auburn-haired man be present if not to mourn? Kenneth had told her Parnell Anderson and his family owned half of Stone Beach. Perhaps he felt obliged to express the town's condolences.

"You have my sincere regrets," he murmured as if he'd read her mind.

Although Sydney fastened onto his flat blue-eyed gaze, she refused to explore it too deeply. Still, getting the distinct feeling he wasn't being up-front with her, she took a step back toward her brother. Dakota tightened an arm around her.

"Sorry we couldn't find the body. That would have helped to put your mind at rest," Brickman added.

Startled speechless by his insincere tone—as if he was saying what was expected of him—she merely stared. Water splashed into her eyes and she realized the drizzle had turned into a steady rain.

Dakota squeezed her shoulders. "Come on, Syd," he urged.

"Thank you both for coming to the service," she murmured, trying not to let her speculations about the men bother her. She needed some rest. Then she would be able to think clearly.

The walk with its painful memories only forty-eight hours old exhausted her. She remembered every rock and tree she had passed in her flight to the house…her last desperate attempt to save Kenneth, even though she'd known it was too late. A front window had been boarded up. She'd broken the glass to let herself in and call for help, but the searchers hadn't found Kenneth's body.

If only they had, she wouldn't have imagined he might still be alive.

EVERY TIME SYDNEY closed her eyes the dreams began. Trapped. Surrounded by fire. Falling. Danger everywhere.

She was exhausted and feeling more fragile than she wanted to admit when the family convened in the living room the following evening. The past three days had been a living nightmare, one from which she wanted to run. But nightmares had the power to follow. So, she would stay, make her peace with herself and settle Kenneth's estate before moving on.

Feeling as if the weight of the world were on her shoulders, she curled up on the couch where she sipped at a brandy Dakota urged her to take. He parked himself in front of a windowed wall and stared out at the gray skies that reflected her own mood.

"You'll feel better once you get to Seattle," Jasper Raferty suddenly announced from the chair opposite the couch.

Sydney realized he meant her. "I'm not going to Seattle. This will be my home for a while."

"She can't stay here alone," Jasper said, looking from his younger daughter who sat on the floor, back to the couch, to his son. "Tell her, Dakota. She listens to you."

"If she wants to stay, that's up to her."

Sydney gave him a grateful half smile. "I want to stay."

"I'll stay with you," Asia volunteered.

Sydney knew her younger sister would stay out of love. She patted Asia's long ash-blond hair, almost silver compared with her own streaked ash-brown. "You've got a shop to run and this is the height of the tourist season."

Asia leaned her head back to the cushion and looked at Sydney from the upside-down position. "Port Townsend can survive without me for a few days. And Jeanne can run the shop."

"You've already been gone for several days," Sydney reminded her. "All of you have lives to get back to, work to do, while I have..."

She didn't want to say any more. She had her memories, as few as they were. And she had to get her life in order.

"I'd like to stay," Asia insisted.

"And I need to be alone."

The ensuing silence lasted mere seconds. Her father coughed and said, "Being alone at a time like this isn't healthy."

"Perhaps it wasn't for you when Mom died." Even though she was nothing like her pragmatic father, Sydney knew he loved her. She tried to soften the statement. "I need to have some quiet time—time to think."

"So you can conjure up a dead man?"

His ready skepticism hurt her even though she was trying to convince herself that she really had imagined things this time—that she'd been reacting to the stress of the situation. Judge Jasper Raferty had never allowed his highly imaginative child to develop what some people considered her "gifts."

And after years of feeling different, alienated, she had suppressed what she eventually felt was a curse. She'd started over, made a new life for herself. But now she was either in the midst of a nervous breakdown or her past was catching up to her. She needed to find out what was happening to her and to deal with the situation. Until she determined this, she would not find happiness for a very long time.

Asia's hand slipped into hers. "Hey, want to go for a walk or something?"

Dry-eyed despite the emotions that welled within her, Sydney scrambled off the couch. "No. I, uh, just need some rest. And I think you should all leave." Hearing her father's sharp intake of breath, she said, "I love you and I thank you for being here, but it's time for you to go. I'll call you in a few days."

Before she could receive more well-intentioned advice, Sydney headed for the guest room she was using. The guest room was lavishly decorated and though she didn't feel comfortable surrounded by an abundance of opulence that bordered on bad taste— the furnishings belonged in a mansion rather than a simple seaside home—she hadn't been able to face the master bedroom that she and Kenneth would have shared.

She wasn't aware that Dakota had followed her upstairs until she was about to close the door.

"Can I come in?"

In silent agreement, she turned from the doorway. "Think I need to be tucked in, do you?"

"Among other things. As I remember, you used to like my bedtime stories."

Sydney made a face. "When I was ten, maybe. In case your memory is failing, I just hit thirty-two."

"I'm still your big brother. And I still love you."

"But?"

"No buts." He turned back the satin quilt. "Get in."

Following orders, Sydney slipped into the ostentatious four-poster. Dakota sat next to her and leaned back against a garishly carved post.

"Once upon a time," he began while stroking her forehead, "there lived a young woman who always felt slightly out of step with the world around her."

"Hey, this isn't really necessary," Sydney told him, immediately discomfited. "Besides, as I remember, you used to tell me horror stories, not fairy tales."

He put a finger over her lips. "Shush. Let me continue. Despite the fact that she was different, this young woman had everything going for her. She was bright, creative, enthusiastic. And most important, she had a heart of gold. Unfortunately, when she finally found someone to share that heart with, she lost him and thought everything was gone."

Unbidden tears sprang to her eyes. "Maybe she was right."

"She was wrong. All she needed was time to heal and—"

"And then everything would be great and she'd live happily ever after. How can you be so sure about the future, Dakota?"

"Because I know you. You're not just a survivor," he said, continuing to stroke her forehead, to relax her in spite of her tightly wound feelings. "You're a winner."

"Of awards, maybe." As the head of an advertising creative team, she'd always been good at creating images. "Awards don't count for much in the long run."

"You're a winner at life, Syd. You've got to believe that. We learn something from loss. We find strength in it and go on."

Dakota knew something of loss himself, Sydney remembered. He'd been madly in love only to be betrayed by the woman. Maureen hadn't died, but a piece of her brother's heart had.

As had a piece of her own.

But Dakota's gentle massage vanquished such unwelcome thoughts from her mind. The stress and sleepless hours of the past days caught up with her and Sydney let herself go....

"SYDNEY...."

She opened her eyes to night. Rather than coming up out of sleep gently, she was startled awake. Kenneth had been calling her to him. Heart pounding, she strained to hear. Nothing.

Had she really heard his voice? Now she lay in the dark, pulse quickened, ears strained, but the only sounds she heard were those of wind and ocean drifting through the open doors that led out to the second-floor deck.

"Kenneth?" she called out.

No answer.

Her throat closed as she realized she must have been dreaming.

Chilled by the damp night air, she rose and closed the outside doors before wandering downstairs where her family had left the lights on. A note on the glass coffee table informed her that Asia had made dinner and all she had to do was throw it in the microwave. Too bad she wasn't hungry.

What to do?

She could watch television, but she might see one of her commercial ads and start remembering the burnout that had taken her away from L.A. And listening to music would remind her of Kenneth's favorite pastimes. What could she do that would lift her spirits?

The tarot cards immediately sprang to mind.

Though she'd consciously suppressed her own psychic abilities for years, Sydney hadn't rejected her interest in cards and crystals. As a source of insight, the Tarot drew her. She rarely did her own readings, but now she was compelled to make an exception. She could ask them if she'd have something to look forward to. Maybe a reading would comfort her.

Getting the cards from her purse, she cleared the coffee table where she began laying them out in the traditional Celtic cross. As usual, she lost herself in concentration and looked for the positive, something she'd always been able to find.

Until now.

Card after card reinforced her anxiety. Swords and more swords, combined with the less positive figures of the Major Arcana, made her view the overall layout unfavorably, despite her wish to do otherwise.

She saw sorrow and separation, which was natural. But treachery and violence? The inability to choose wisely in an important matter? Her immediate past—the Fool reversed—indicated faulty thinking. While the future showed no way out of present difficulties, the Knight of Swords implied an aggressive, dark-haired stranger was about to rush headlong into her life. The Five of Swords realized her greatest fear—that she was a threat to herself.

Was she going out of her mind, then?

Reluctantly, she flipped over the last card, the X-factor. The Lovers. She glanced back at the dark-haired stranger. The Knight must be Kenneth.

But her love was dead, wasn't he?

Perhaps she was meant to join him. . . .

Sydney told herself she was being ridiculous. The cards were subject to personal interpretation; naturally her mood must be coloring her reading.

Still, unable to help feeling nervous, she decided to take a walk. Fresh air would clear her head. She didn't bother to gather up the cards before pulling on a long-sleeved cotton sweater and putting on walking shoes. Leaving the house lit, she locked the door behind her and set off across the grounds.

The ocean called to her, but rather than retrace the path Kenneth had chosen, she headed in the opposite direction, north toward the beach that led to town. The going was easy—no scrambling over rocks. At the far edge of the property, a sloped path led down to the hard-packed sand strip. As she descended, fog rose from the water. Ghostly fingers slithered along the ground and wrapped themselves around her ankles and calves. She glanced back over her shoulder. The lit house was merely a hazy beacon in the distance.

She kept going, increasing her pace and trying to separate herself from the tragedy that would be part of her forever, while the fog danced around her like a shroud.

When the moon slid behind a bank of clouds, and darkness blanketed her surroundings, Sydney glanced back again. The house had been swallowed by the murky night. She should have taken a flashlight. Unsure of how far she'd gone, of how she would get back through the inky darkness, she stopped. Waves lapped the shore to her left, the sound deadened by the fog. She could see the vague outline of the hill that rose steeply to her right. Ahead, tiny glimmers pinpointed town buildings and urged her forward. From there, she could follow the paved road back to the house.

Was it her imagination or did she suddenly hear a scrabbling noise...footsteps...a soft expulsion of breath?

A glance over her shoulder proved nothing. The fog was too dense, the night too dark, her senses too confused. She shoved balled fists into jeans' pockets, hunched into her sweater and hurried.

Sydney....

Her name whispered eerily on the wind, sending a chill up her spine. Unable to decide from which direction it had come, she turned full circle. No matter how hard she tried she couldn't see farther than a few feet. She strained to hear. Nothing. Of course, she was imagining things.

Continuing on, however, she felt ill at ease. She sensed another presence nearby. She rushed forward, tripped over something. Hands flashed out of her pockets. Her palms scraped the rough bark of a log half buried in the sand. Before she could get to her feet, she heard the voice again.

"*Sydney....*"

Kenneth's voice.

Hands groping to avoid crashing into other obstacles, she rose and stumbled away from the voice, away from the presence. She choked back a sob, told herself she wasn't going crazy. Wanting contact with a loved one was only natural. She hadn't yet let go, that was all. There was no presence. No voice. Only her desperate wish to wake up from a living nightmare.

Then why was she so frightened?

"Sydney, my love...."

A strangled sound escaped her as she ran blindly through the fog. Her feet hit water, splashed, and she knew she was going in the wrong direction. Confused. She slowed down and veered away from the heavy smell of the ocean and headed directly for those pinpoints of light. She didn't want to join Kenneth in his watery grave.

Sydney.... Her name so soft it might have been the wind sighing.

She couldn't help herself. She began to sob. Control gusted away. She couldn't stop crying, couldn't stop the rush of her pulse that surged through every limb. She still could hear her name echoing faintly through her mind. What was happening to her? She had to get away from the ocean with its terrifying memories.

Get away from the dream.

Glowing lights meant people, civilization, someone to talk to. Sydney shuddered with relief as she got control of herself and slowed down, throwing one last look back into the ocean's shroud. As she sought the lights ahead, she was slammed to a stop by something solid—something that was neither rock nor tree. She steadied herself on well-muscled arms. The arms of a man.

Kenneth?

Breath caught in her throat, making her force out the words, "Is that really you?"

Chapter Two

Benno DeMartino steadied the frantic-sounding woman. "Whoa, you've got the wrong guy."

Making a choked sound, she pulled away from him. "S-sorry. I thought you were someone else. I forgot my flashlight and couldn't see clearly."

"I guess not."

Benno snapped on his own torch and shone it on the woman. It didn't take much insight to realize she was terrified and on the verge of collapse. Her distress was written on her face and dramatized in her posture. Shoulders hunched, she seemed about to shrink into herself.

"Are there stairs or something around here so I can get up to the road?" she asked.

"Not too far from here. I was just heading back into town," he lied, having only set foot on the beach moments ago.

He'd just gotten back into town an hour earlier and had meant to lose himself in the solitary night for a while—something he'd done most of his life when troubled—but this woman's problems seemed monumental compared with his own. Doing a good deed

wouldn't hurt him; after all, he didn't have that many
to his credit.

Holding up the flashlight, he said, "We can share."

"Thanks."

As he started off, she fell into step with him. Although she didn't come too close, her tension vibrated through the space between them. He could
smell fear on a person and this lady was definitely
afraid. He knew every resident of Stone Beach and
since she wasn't one of them, he reckoned she must be
a tourist. But why had she been out alone on the beach
at night? He was too aware of a person's need for privacy to question her motives.

When they got to a part of the embankment that
wasn't too steep, he asked, "Think you can make it up
here if I give you a hand? Or should we keep going
until we get to the stairs?"

Nervously, she glanced over her shoulder as if she
were looking for, yet dreading, meeting up with the
man for whom he'd been mistaken. "Here."

He climbed halfway up and held out his hand. She
hesitated only a second before taking it. Some people
trusted too easily, he thought, helping her up over the
sand hill. The moment she set foot on level ground,
however, she withdrew her hand. Still far from the
main beach area, they stood in a paved cul-de-sac, a
turnaround area for residents at the south end of town.

Benno flashed his light over the young woman once
more. Her short hair was damp. Thick tendrils were
plastered to a broad forehead and rounded cheeks,
which gave her something of a baby face. She was
shivering, but from chill or fright? Maybe both.

"You look as though you could use something to
warm up your insides." Benno found it amazingly easy

to be kind to this stranger. That she might disappear into the night as quickly as she had materialized disturbed him. "Can I buy you a cup of coffee? A drink? Tea?"

"Tea sounds good."

She seemed relieved, as if she didn't want to be alone. He could identify with that feeling.

"I know just the place," he said, lightly settling his hand on her elbow. He led her past his wind-battered cottage, which overlooked the beach. She'd probably get the wrong idea if he invited her into his home. "Since we're going to share a cup of tea, we shouldn't be strangers. I'm Benno DeMartino."

"Sydney Raferty L—. Uh, Raferty."

She'd been about to add another name. He wondered what she'd been about to say, but he didn't press her. They walked in silence, and, as if his mere presence was comforting to her, he sensed the lady was beginning to relax. Odd how some people could relate to people they barely knew. He himself had difficulty feeling comfortable with strangers, though Sydney Raferty might prove to be the exception. Something about her drew his interest—and as odd as it seemed, his protective instincts as well. Considering his background, that was saying a lot for her.

As they left the eerie night beach behind, the fog thinned and the lights of Main Street glowed dimly overhead.

"We're almost there." He snapped off his flashlight as they crossed the street. "So, how do you like Stone Beach?"

"I don't know." Forehead furrowed, Sydney looked around at the deserted shop-lined street. "I really haven't had the chance to see much of anything. It seems nice.''

"Stone Beach is pretty laid-back. Quiet. Not like Seaside or Astoria," he said, referring to larger nearby towns. "We have a number of artists and writers living here."

"Which are you?"

Benno laughed. "Neither." He stopped in front of a wooden building, the large windows of which were darkened. A Closed sign hung in the glassed front door. "This is the place."

"But it's locked up tight." She sounded disappointed.

"Ah, but I have the key." He produced it with a flourish and unlocked the door.

Sydney looked up at the shingle which hung overhead. *"Benno's Place?"*

"Benno DeMartino, proprietor, at your service." He flicked a light switch just inside the door and held out a hand indicating she should enter. When she hesitated, he preceded her and called over his shoulder. "Come on in. You have the distinction of being my only customer of the evening."

Stools were stacked upside down on the bar, as were the chairs on the tables. The place had a neglected air, though he'd only been gone for a week.

He headed for the bar where he righted a couple of stools before starting water for the tea. He heard Sydney's light footsteps on the wooden floor but he chose not to engage her in conversation immediately. Instead, he rinsed out a couple of mugs and set an Almond Enchantment tea bag in each. The young woman was taking her time looking around, he noticed. Perhaps she was using his surroundings to decide who he was.

If so, she was as foolish as most of the locals. Poster-covered salmon-colored walls, wooden tables and chairs and a small stage with accompanying mike and speakers wouldn't tell her who he was as a person. He looked up to find her staring at him, her expression curious.

"I've been out of town and the place has been locked up," he found himself telling her. "I just got back tonight." He was caught by her odd gray eyes, large and round and filled with sadness. "So, are you staying in a motel or visiting friends?"

"Neither, exactly." The distraught expression assaulted her face once more, though she was visibly trying to control herself from giving in to what was bothering her. "I'm here alone now."

Alone and lonely, Benno thought. And afraid. He couldn't forget that. Why? A top-notch bartender could get anyone to open up.

"Want to come sit over here at the bar or would you prefer one of the tables?" he asked.

"The bar is fine."

He slid her mug toward her as she slipped onto one of the stools. "I get the feeling you could use something stronger than plain tea." He lifted a bottle of amaretto from the shelf behind him. "How about it?" When she nodded, Benno splashed a shot into her mug. He waited until she took a couple of sips before asking, "Planning on staying long?"

"I'm not sure. A while, I guess."

She seemed distant—almost alienated—something he himself had experienced more often than was good for a person. "Since you don't know anyone in town,

I'd be glad to help make you feel at home," he heard himself offering before he'd had a chance to think it over.

"That's very kind of you." Sydney's knuckles whitened on the mug and she suddenly said, "The reason I don't know anyone in town is because my new husband brought me here on our wedding day...and then he died."

No wonder she was so distraught. So when she'd bumped into Benno she thought *he* was her dead husband? The realization gave Benno a start though he supposed it wasn't all that unusual for someone who'd recently lost a loved one to fall prey to wishful thinking. Still, the kind of fear she'd displayed didn't seem to go hand in hand with love and hope.

"I still can't believe Kenneth is dead," she whispered.

Kenneth? Benno's mind raced. Sydney had run into him on the strip of beach south of town. Only one man by that name lived along the cliffs. His breath came short and he stiffened.

"Your husband—" he forced himself to complete the unthinkable "—he wasn't Kenneth Lord, was he?"

"Yes," she said, confirming his fear. "You knew him?"

"Knew him?" Benno felt as if he'd been smacked in the gut. Kenneth dead? It wasn't possible. He gripped the edge of the bar so tightly his fingers went numb. "He was my friend. I'm sorry. My God, how did it happen?"

Sydney took a sip of tea as if to bolster herself. "A horrible accident. He fell from the cliff near the house."

"Kenneth wasn't clumsy. This is unbeliev-able...unthinkable!" He stared at her. "Were you with him?"

"I was back a ways taking his picture. One minute he was posing for me...the next he was gone. Drowned."

That information gave Benno the weirdest feeling. Another drowning. Coincidence?

Grief for his friend made him reach for a whiskey bottle. He poured a shot and downed it straight. As if the fire could burn away the shock and disbelief. God, not Kenneth, not his only friend in a town that had always seemed alien to him. He and Kenneth had a bond no one and nothing could break.

Nothing but death, he thought, shocked to the core.

He stared at the window. No wonder he'd been drawn to Sydney. Somehow, his lifelong bond with Kenneth Lord had spilled over to include the man's wife.

A stranger.

Something didn't gel here. He gave her an even harder look.

"Kenneth never told me he was getting married. I had no idea that he was seriously involved with some-one."

"It was one of those storybook romances," she said with irony. "Love at first sight, whirlwind courtship, impulsive marriage. Too bad there was no happy end-ing."

Kenneth must have met her while he was out of town. "He was a good friend, too young to die at thirty-seven."

"We, uh, held his memorial service yesterday," Sydney said.

"Memorial—no funeral?"

Her eyes filled as she shook her head. "The search team couldn't find his body."

The fact unsettled Benno once more. A corpse should have been beached with the incoming tide—as he well knew—if not here, then somewhere along the coast. And it had already been three days. . . .

"They may find him yet, Sydney," he said in an effort to comfort her. Without having actually seen a body, she undoubtedly had no sense of finality to the relationship. Hell, he couldn't believe it himself.

"Unless Kenneth really isn't dead."

That gave him a start. "What?"

"I don't know what to believe."

"Just because no body was found—"

"I know," she interrupted. "I've heard all the rationalizations in the world. My family is rather pragmatic when it comes to the unexplained. But . . ."

"But?"

Sydney shook her head. "You wouldn't believe me, either. You'd think I was losing it. Maybe I am," she mumbled. "I thought I could stay in Kenneth's house alone, but the place got to me. I took a walk to make myself feel better." She licked a drop of tea from her bottom lip. "I, uh, thought I heard his voice out there in the foggy night. He only died three days ago and I guess I still haven't come to terms with losing him," she said, an embarrassed note in her voice.

Benno sensed there was even more to her story than she was sharing, but he was too distraught by the news to figure out what. "Because you thought you heard a voice?"

She nodded, swallowed hard, and said, "Added to a premonition that Kenneth was still alive and waiting for me to slip into his arms."

"Wishful thinking."

Sydney laughed, but there was no humor in the sound. "Yes. I guess that's a more acceptable explanation than being crazy." She took a sip from the mug and placed it on the bar with a clunk that had a ring of finality. "Thanks for the flashlight and the tea, Benno. I think I'll be going now."

"Wait." His hand slid over hers and held it fast. "You're upset. Let me see you safely home."

"No, really—"

"I insist. Let me do this for Kenneth. For my friend."

She didn't argue and he could tell that, whether or not she was willing to admit it, Sydney needed someone to lean on. His shoulder was stronger than some and it happened to be available. And in helping her, he was doing what he could for a friend. Probably the last thing anyone could do for Kenneth.

He picked up the flashlight and circled the bar. "Come on. My car is down the street."

He felt her reluctance as she followed him outside. Benno didn't know why he had this bizarre impulse to play knight-in-shining-armor to her maiden-in-distress, but something about Sydney got to him at a gut level. Maybe it was the eyes. An odd pale gray, they managed to look right through him one minute and reveal her vulnerability the next.

Despite what the locals still thought of him, he'd always been a sucker for hurt or lost creatures . . . and right now, Sydney Raferty Lord was about as hurt and lost as a human being could get.

AS THEY SPED ALONG the curved, hilly road in a low-slung '67 Thunderbird convertible, the top up against the chilly night, Sydney glanced at the man who claimed to have been Kenneth's friend, and wondered why Benno DeMartino was going out of his way for a stranger.

Buttoned to the throat, his black shirt complemented his dark good looks and further allowed him to meld with the night. Stubble brushed his olive skin except for the naked scar on his chin, and a diamond stud winked from his ear. When oncoming headlights flashed through the T-bird's interior, she could see his granitelike profile framed by longish black hair slicked back and tied in a short ponytail at the nape of his neck. His sharp, rugged features made him appear eternally skeptical.

And yet Benno had been so kind to her.

He didn't know anything about her. She sighed. Piercing light brown eyes flashed at her and made her turn away self-consciously. She wondered why Kenneth hadn't ever mentioned Benno.

She stared out at the fog-shrouded shoreline but saw no lights ahead. She did not look forward to spending the night at the house alone. Sydney guessed she should have let Asia have her way and stay, but for once, she hadn't bent under the force of her younger sister's personality. Her mistake. Now she would have only herself for company.

She wondered if Benno could read her thoughts when he commented, "So you're alone at the house. What about Martha? Did she go back to Portland so soon?"

"Martha doesn't even know her brother is... She doesn't know anything about the accident. She doesn't even know about the marriage."

"Kenneth didn't want her at the wedding?" He sounded incredulous.

"I told you we married impulsively. There was no time to send out invitations."

"He could have made a phone call and Martha would have come running. She was his only real family."

"Yes, I know," Sydney said, trying not to sound too hostile. Benno was merely being curious, not critical. "He told me their parents died years ago."

"Did he also tell you he was fourteen years older than his sister, as much a father to her as a brother?" Without waiting for her affirmative reply, he muttered, "They were so close, I can't believe he didn't want her at the wedding."

"It wasn't like that. Really. And I—I tried to get in touch with her after... the accident." Sydney clasped her hands together tightly as if that would prevent her from breaking down. "No answer, so I left a message on her answering machine. Such a cold way of giving someone bad news. So impersonal. I didn't know what else to do."

Voice sounding more kind than critical, Benno said, "You were caught in the middle of a rather exceptional situation."

Were? That smacked of the past, and, as far as Sydney was concerned, she was still caught. At the moment, she wasn't sure how she was going to resolve anything. Neither Kenneth's death, nor her own life.

Benno slowed the Thunderbird and she realized that they had arrived at the house. Looking out at it, she frowned. "What's going on? I left lights on all over the house." Now only the living room glowed through the downstairs windows.

"Are you sure?"

"Positive. I even remember seeing the windows lit when I was walking along the beach."

Benno grabbed his flashlight from the back seat where he'd tossed it. "I'll come in with you and look around."

Sydney didn't try to talk him out of it. She was suddenly as much on edge as she'd been when she'd fled the house earlier. But no one answered when he called out, and a thorough search revealed no sign of an intruder. Things were as she had left them.

Everything but the lights.

"I—I don't understand. I was sure..." She shook her head and decided not to complete her thought. "Forget about it." She had to remember how stressed she'd been. But upset enough to have forgotten turning off several light switches? She didn't want to dwell on the thought. And she didn't want to be alone, not just yet. "It's my turn to offer you a drink."

Benno gave her an odd look and studied her closely for an uncomfortable moment. She shifted under his scrutiny. She wondered if he thought she was going crazy?

"Listen, Sydney, if you want some company in the house, I could stay." He nodded to the sleek black leather sofa. "I could sack out for the night down here."

"I couldn't ask you to do that," she said, even though the offer of company was tempting. "Besides, it's not necessary. I can take care of myself."

"I'm sure you can. But the offer's still open. I have a thing for sleeping on other peoples' couches. Really."

When she saw his smile, Sydney realized he was teasing her. And she realized that she was smiling, too. A rush of warmth passed between them and she knew she wouldn't turn down his kind offer. He was a stranger and she should probably be wary, but she relied on her instincts that told her he was a trustworthy person.

"Thanks."

His smile widened to a grin. "If I have a crick in my back in the morning, though, I may ask you to walk on it."

"You're really into torture, huh?"

"Nah, just creative living."

They both laughed. Sydney knew she'd made the right decision.

"There are sheets and a quilt and pillows in there," she said, pointing to the window seat topped with a leather pad that her brother Dakota had discovered when he'd slept on the couch the night before. "I'll clear my things away."

About to remove the tarot cards from the coffee table, she froze when she noticed the loose card that lay across the middle of the spread. Added to the other negative vibes she'd gotten from the reading, this one chilled her. Death, one of the most powerful images of the Tarot, wasn't necessarily to be taken literally. But loss of hope and major changes could be almost as frightening, and the fact that she hadn't dealt the card, that it had somehow worked its way into her reading gave her the creeps.

She must have flipped it over by accident when she'd set down the deck, Sydney told herself.

"So, you're into reading tarot cards."

Right behind her, Benno made her jump. "Aah!"

"Whoa," he said, steadying her for the second time that night. "I didn't mean to startle you. So, did you find out anything interesting about yourself?"

Not about to tell him that her reading had been the reason for her flight from the house—nor about the appearance of an extra card that might have slipped from the deck without her noticing—Sydney gathered the cards together. She hoped he didn't notice her hands were shaking as she slipped the cards into their pouch.

"Reading the Tarot is always interesting," she said earnestly, at the same time trying to regulate the thumping of her heart. She stuck the pouch into her purse, which she'd left on the floor. "You can get new insights into yourself. Sort of self-analysis, using both what you know about yourself and also being open to interpretation."

"Will you read mine sometime?"

"If you like." She backed away from him and threw the purse onto a chair. "Um, I'm going to warm up some milk for myself..."

"Not my speed," Benno told her. "Do you mind if I help myself to something stronger?"

"I would have suggested that if only I could figure out where the stuff is hidden. My brother found some brandy yesterday."

"The bar is over here," Benno said, walking to the teak unit that lined the only wall breaking up the downstairs living area. He opened a drop leaf on one side that revealed a well-stocked bar. "I've been around enough in the past few months to know where things are."

"Help yourself." Sydney escaped to the kitchen area that was separated from the rest of the downstairs by the cabineted wall on one side and a half wall that formed a breakfast bar on the other.

She removed a copper pot from a cast iron hanger, which had been installed above the work island, and set it on the stove. Glass against glass clinked from the other side of the wall as Benno helped himself to his drink.

She couldn't help asking, "What was he like?"

"Who? Kenneth? You married the man."

"I met him all of two weeks ago. I could hardly have any in-depth knowledge of him in such a short time." Hoping Benno wasn't going to tell her what he thought of the impulsive marriage, Sydney opened the refrigerator door.

"Kenneth was probably one of the most talented men I've ever met," Benno told her, his voice drifting closer. "He designed this house."

"I didn't know that. I mean, I knew he was an architect, but he didn't tell me about the house. I guess he would have if he'd . . ."

Sydney chose not to complete the statement.

She removed the quart of milk from the refrigerator and turned toward the stove. A part of her still thought Kenneth was alive and waiting for her to find him. That same part viewed the past few days as a bad dream from which she was still trying to awaken.

Suddenly feeling Benno's presence on the other side of the island, she looked up to find him staring at her hand—and her naked ring finger?—as she poured milk into the pot. She didn't feel obliged to explain what had happened to the ring, but she wondered if he'd understand her actions in sacrificing the love token to the sea.

"I'm not as interested in the professional side of Kenneth as I am in the private side of him," she explained as she turned on the burner. "The friend. The brother."

Expression thoughtful, Benno took a swig of the amber liquid in his glass. "Your late husband was as trustworthy and loyal a friend as a man could ask for. And he was certainly a better brother than Martha deserved."

Startled by the unexpected criticism, Sydney asked, "What do you mean?"

"I mean Martha was a spoiled kid, a highly spoiled teenager and an even more spoiled young woman. She always got what she wanted . . . one way or another."

"I thought you liked her."

"I never said that." Leaning on the counter, he rolled the glass between his hands and stared down into the liquid. "I was merely surprised that Martha didn't show for the wedding. She took advantage of outward appearances when it came to pleasing or placating Kenneth since he controlled her purse strings."

Indignant at his conclusion, Sydney snapped, "Maybe she tried to please him because she loved him."

Benno merely raised his thick dark eyebrows and pointed to her milk. "You're about to boil over."

She took the opportunity to let the conversation drop. She didn't want to hear unflattering things about Kenneth's family.

After pouring the milk into a glass, she set the pot in the sink. "I think I'll go up to bed."

"I'm ready to sack out myself," Benno said, tipping his own glass toward her in salute.

Sydney moved around the island and through the living-room area toward the stairs opposite the front door. He followed only as far as the couch. She sipped at her milk as she took the first several steps, then paused halfway up to the balcony that overlooked the open two-story living room.

"Benno..."

Standing over the couch where he'd unfolded a sheet, he paused to look up at her. "What?"

Somehow, his having done such a domestic task seemed incongruous with the image she had of him. He seemed rugged and mysterious and a little dangerous. Funny how he also made her feel so safe.

"Thanks."

He stared at her, his expression serious, his eyes piercing. "Yell if you need me."

"Sure." She tried to smile but failed.

Sydney finished climbing the stairs to her room where she set the half-empty glass on the gilt-edged white nightstand. Kenneth had laughed at her nighttime habit, but she'd explained that she found drinking warm milk helped her relax when she was anxious.

The milk was doing its job even as she changed into her cotton nightgown. Her mind began to drift. Slipping through the lace curtains around the bed, she sank into it and pulled up the satin quilt. One last sip of milk. She adjusted the table lamp so that only a soft light within the frosted glass body glowed.

Sydney realized she wouldn't be feeling so relaxed if Benno wasn't downstairs. His dark visage was the

last thing she saw before her conscious mind gave way
to the mysteries of the night....

SYDNEY....

Sometime later she stirred, reluctant to surface from
the warm cocoon of sleep that enveloped her, yet
drawn by the voice in her head. She turned restlessly,
her fingers clenching and unclenching around the
corner of the quilt.

So sleepy... why was Kenneth trying to wake her?

Sydney, my love....

The eerie sound whispered through her. She moaned
in protest, tried to drive away the disturbing voice.
Flipping to her other side, she got tangled in the covers but didn't have the will to fight them. Dressed in
his yellow shirt, Kenneth stood waiting for her.

Another dream. How many more?

Sydney, my love, I'm waiting. Come to me.

Half-awake now, she felt desperate to stop the
agonizing fantasies. Her eyes flew open to a darkened
room and she tried to get her bearings. Although she
felt hazy and disoriented, she pushed herself up on her
elbows and tried to focus on her surroundings.

Her jaw fell slack at the apparition before her.

Arms extended in welcome, a figure was silhouet-
ted in the doorway leading out to the deck. A man
wearing a yellow shirt.

"Kenneth!"

The room began whirling. She closed her eyes,
rubbed them and looked again. Nothing. Gone. He
wasn't really there. Another dream? Or an illusion?

Seconds later she realized the room shouldn't be
pitch-black.

Her pulse quickened.

"Sydney."

From beyond the open double doors came a whisper that had to be real.

"Kenneth?"

A breeze swept through the room in answer. And one of the outside storm shutters banged against its frame, startling her even more. The doors to the deck were open. She hadn't touched them before going to bed, had she? Trying to remember as she sat up, Sydney felt the room float around her. While her head was light, her hand was heavy when she fumbled for the switch to the table lamp.

Something that sounded like metal skittered across the surface of the nightstand. Her hand shot out after the object and, in the process, nicked the glass, making it crash to the floor.

"Damn!"

Finally Sydney found the switch. The soft light caught the object that lay near the edge of the nightstand.

A ring.

Heart pounding, she retrieved it. Nuggeted outside, smooth inside. Her ring. Impossible. Hers was at the bottom of the ocean. She ran a fingertip inside the circle and felt a faint etching. Turning the ring to the light, she strained her eyes to read the inscription, but her eyes wouldn't focus properly. She squeezed her lids shut, then tried again.

Kenneth loves Sydney.

"Oh, my God! Kenneth!" she cried.

She scrambled out of bed, but her knees wouldn't hold her.

"Sydney...."

The voice came from beyond the porch, from the fog-shrouded grounds. She had to get there, had to get to Kenneth. Why wouldn't her legs cooperate? The room seemed to be heaving. Fiercely, she clutched the ring and forced her legs to move toward the open doors. She heard a banging noise somewhere but she could no more focus her mind on the sound than on anything else.

"Kenneth, where are you?" she called, bursting out onto the deck in confusion.

"Sydney?" Both voice and noise sounded closer.

She forced her feet to move, caught a glimpse of someone below in the fog. A shadowy figure...

"Sydney!"

Behind her, the voice made her whirl around. She lost her balance and flew back hard against the wooden rail that shrieked from the jarring weight. The ring went flying—followed by Sydney, her face a mask of horror.

Chapter Three

Hands of steel hooked onto Sydney's hips, jerking her to a stop. Her upper body free-floated, still out of control. Her stomach somersaulted and her heart threatened to burst through the wall of her chest as she dangled, torso arched and upside down. The night whirled around her head while wood bit into her buttocks and a human vise trapped her legs. Precariously balanced on the balcony's rail, she could still fall. She'd fallen in her dreams....

Blood rushed to her head. Mouth dry, she croaked, "Help."

"That's what I'm trying to do, Sydney. Come on, lift your arms and grab hold of mine."

Concentrating, she forced herself to respond to the deep voice. Hands slid to her waist and steadied her. She caught hold of thick, powerfully muscled wrists.

"That's it," the voice urged. "Now hang on. Steady."

Her body was shifted forward to safety. The vise relaxed and freed her. Her feet touched the deck. But the face that gradually came into focus by the soft glow of light coming from the bedroom was rough-hewn and beard-stubbled. Confused, she frowned.

"Benno?"

"I'm here."

She glanced over her shoulder and the fog danced in slow motion. "Did you see him? Kenneth?"

He gave her a sharp shake that got her full attention. "It's not Kenneth, Sydney. It's Benno."

"I know who you are. I mean out there," she said, slanting her head. The landscape shifted and it took a monumental effort to make the world stop moving. No matter how hard Sydney tried, she could see nothing beyond the foggy blanket still rising from the cliffs that overlooked the ocean. "I heard Kenneth call me."

"Sydney, listen." Firm fingers under her chin brought her face-to-face with the man who had just saved her life. "I was calling you. Not Kenneth. There was a crash and then I heard you cry out. You must have been dreaming."

Dreaming? Had she been? Sydney had thought so, but now she wasn't certain.

"I found my wedding ring," she ground out. Even talking was an effort. "I threw it into the ocean at the memorial service so it would be with Kenneth forever. When I woke up a little while ago, the ring was on the nightstand." Not liking the way Benno was frowning at her, she insisted, "Don't look at me that way. I didn't imagine it." At least she didn't think so.

"So where is this ring?"

She looked down at her empty hand. "I—I dropped it down there somewhere." Hadn't she?

Sydney was so dizzy she could hardly stand upright. And her mouth was dry, as though she had a hangover. But she'd only had that splash of amaretto in her tea and that had been a good while ago. Her eyes demanded to close, her brain to shut out the all-consuming feeling of helplessness. This was not her, not Sydney Raferty, not the strong self-assured woman she knew herself to be. She'd been losing herself little by little over the past months and the feeling of helplessness was intensifying.

What in the world was happening to her?

That she'd just been saved from a possibly fatal fall broke down the last of her defenses. Letting go of her reserve, she began to sob.

"You're going to be all right," Benno assured her, and when she shook her head in protest, he pulled her into his arms. "Shush, I'm here and you're safe now."

Safe.

She clung to his shirtfront as his strong arms wrapped around her. Tears continued to fall from her eyes. Safe. How could she be safe from her own mind when it kept playing tricks on her? She must have dreamed everything.

But the ring—it had been so real!

Benno's hand stroking her head relaxed her and, grateful that she wasn't alone, Sydney melted into him, allowed him to comfort her. If it wasn't for him, she might have fallen to her death. She owed him her life. But how would she ever repay the kindness of this stranger?

When her tears finally subsided, he said, "Come on, let's get you back to bed."

No protest passed her lips, but when she tried to move, she stumbled. Before she knew what was happening, Benno had lifted her into his arms and carried her inside. She could hear his heart beating strongly through the thickly muscled wall of his chest. When he set her down, she felt bereft. But he didn't immediately leave her side. He settled her into bed and tucked the covers around her.

She took his hand before he could draw away. "I don't know how to thank you."

"You already have. Try to get some rest now."

Still she didn't let go. Realizing that she needed reassurance, Benno sat at the edge of the bed and waited.

"Do you think I'm crazy?" she whispered.

"I think you're exhausted and grief-stricken."

"And confused," she added softly. "If I can't figure out what's going on, how can I expect you to understand? Everything seems so out-of-sync, so fuzzy."

He wondered if she hadn't taken something—a tranquilizer or a sleeping pill—to relax her. That would account for her confusion.

"Everything will be a little less frightening in the morning," he promised with an encouraging grin.

A corresponding smile transformed her ordinary face into something of quiet beauty. "Why do I believe you?"

"Because you need to. Now go back to sleep."

Trustingly, she allowed her drooping eyes to close. Even though she was drifting off, she clutched his hand as if she were hanging on to a lifeline. He didn't have the heart to pull away from her. A wave of tenderness washed through him as he studied her—hurt, vulnerable, fragile.

Her long lashes had separated into wet spikes and a puddle created by her tears lay in the hollow between lid and cheek. Using his thumb, he wiped the moisture away. She stirred, but her breathing deepened as if his touch had relaxed her farther into sleep. She seemed so delicate, but Benno guessed that wasn't unusual under the circumstances.

No, he didn't think she was crazy; she was over-stressed and in need of a friend. When her grip on him loosened, he gently pulled his hand free, snatched the extra pillow and made himself a makeshift bed on the floor. If she were to awaken while caught up in another dream, he would be there for her.

Benno knew what it was like to be alone and afraid. Not much time had passed since he'd left town in disgrace; he could remember it as if it were yesterday. Perhaps the circumstances surrounding that twenty-year-old tragedy made him feel responsible for Kenneth Lord's widow.

Then, again, maybe the link had nothing to do with his friend but with Sydney herself.

As Benno settled down for the night, he started thinking about the circumstances of Kenneth's demise. Death by drowning. Coincidence? How could he ever be sure? One thing was certain—he'd be smart to start looking over his own shoulder.

SYDNEY AWOKE to the brilliance of morning and the sharp smells of freshly brewed coffee and frying bacon.

But who...?

Benno. Hazily, she remembered the man tucking the covers under her chin and then...nothing.

She gazed over the side of the bed at the floor next to the nightstand. The broken glass was gone as was the spilled milk. Benno must have cleaned up quietly so as not to awaken her.

Her empty stomach prompted her to dress in record time. Then, she ran a brush through her short hair. She realized her head was achy, her mouth dry. The hangover feeling stayed with her as she quietly descended the stairs and found an incongruous sight in the kitchen.

"Morning," he said without turning around. "I was about to wake you. Sleep well?"

"No more bad dreams, if that's what you mean." Though she was still feeling hazy and moving in slow motion.

In full daylight, her dark knight seemed even more masculine and wild-looking than she'd remembered. The scar on his chin was more vivid in his beard-stubbled face, his tied-back hair more slick, his rugged features more formidable. But how dangerous could a man with a frying pan in one hand, a spatula in the other, be?

Smothering a grin in the guise of a yawn, she approached and asked, "What can I do to help?"

"Set the table out there." He crooked his dark head toward the deck off the kitchen.

Plates, cups and silverware were already stacked on the counter. Gathering the items to her, she used her hip to pop open the screen door. Benno was close behind with a coffeepot and platter of bacon, eggs and toast.

Once she'd gotten a few bites of food into her stomach, Sydney felt physically better, though she couldn't say the same for her emotions. But her head had cleared and she could appreciate the beauty of the crisp morning. The sun shone strongly, brightening the landscaped grounds for the first time since she'd arrived in Stone Beach. She could hear the ocean stir in the distance and was aware of its distinctive salt scent.

Benno, however, wasn't focusing on their surroundings. His light brown eyes were stuck on her.

"What are you staring at?" she asked, fascinated by the way the diamond stud in his ear winked when he cocked his head.

"You. You look like a different person this morning."

"Must be the good night's sleep you made sure I got," she stated, putting a forkful of eggs into her mouth.

"Don't go all gooey on me again, okay?"

Gooey obviously made the man uncomfortable. "All right. Be modest. You already know how I feel."

His forehead furrowed as he asked, "This is probably none of my business, but I was wondering what you were on last night."

Sydney washed the food down with a mouthful of coffee. "What do you mean—on?"

"I wondered what you took to fall asleep."

"Milk, remember?" At his disbelieving expression she added, "A great tonic for stress."

Benno threw his fork down onto his plate. "Come on, Sydney, you had more than milk in your system. Admit it."

"Right. Amaretto. You're the one who poured the stuff into my mug," she said, a little irritated by the third degree.

"Neither that small shot I gave you nor any number of glasses of warm milk would make you feel disoriented. And you were out of it when I caught up to you, Sydney, badly so."

"I wake up and think I hear and see my dead husband—of course I was confused!"

"I'm not accusing you of anything, and I'm not trying to judge you, so don't get your back up," Benno said calmly. "It's just that doctors are sometimes too generous with sedatives."

"No doctor gave me anything of the kind," she snapped; even though she once more wondered why she should have felt so hung over this morning.

Sydney realized he still wasn't convinced. Getting more aggravated by the moment, she was about to tell him she didn't even know a doctor in the area when she heard a vehicle approach.

"Hmm, a visitor," Benno stated. "Expecting anyone?"

"No. Maybe they found Kenneth."

Breakfast and conversation forgotten, Sydney was through the house in a flash. Indeed, when she opened the front door, the police car was the first thing she saw. The white Porsche behind it the second. A sleek young woman in a fire-engine red silk sundress swung her long legs out of the sports car and set her strappy red-sandaled feet onto the pavement. Officer Mick Brickman almost tripped over his own feet trying to help her alight.

"Well, well, at last," Benno murmured from behind Sydney. "The chicken has come home to roost."

Sydney stared at Martha Lord. The young woman's only resemblance to her older brother was in the cloud of curly, dark brown hair that framed her face. Where Kenneth's features were chiseled and beautiful in a masculine way, Martha's were merely sharp. She clung to Brickman's arm and stared. Her deep-set, dark brown eyes narrowed unattractively as they flicked over Sydney's black spandex knee-length pants, black T-shirt and loose black and fluorescent green striped top that exposed one shoulder and most of the other.

Tone hostile, she said, "So you're the little tramp who claims to have married my brother. What did you do to him?"

Sydney was appalled—and speechless. Undaunted by the lack of response, the woman continued her diatribe.

"You must have plotted to get at Kenneth's money. Don't think you're going to get away—"

"Martha," Benno cut in smoothly as he set a protective hand on Sydney's shoulder, "I see you're in top viper form this morning."

The young woman gazed up at the officer and demanded, "Brick, what the hell is *he* doing here?"

"I don't know," the policeman answered, straightening his pants under his paunch. "What are you doing here, DeMartino? Consoling the widow so soon?"

Flushing at the inference, Sydney was about to tell him off when she felt Benno's fingers tense on her shoulder.

"Mr. DeMartino is here at my invitation, Officer Brickman. Is that a problem for you?"

"Maybe." Brickman's eyebrows furrowed, deepening the puffy bags under his small gray-blue eyes. "You oughta be careful about who you associate with."

She assured him, "Don't worry. I choose my friends carefully."

"And your husband? I mean, supposed husband." Martha corrected herself. Dragging Brickman by the arm, she pushed her way past Sydney and Benno and through the front door of the house. "Come on. I want to look around to see if anything is missing."

"How dare you!" Sydney cried, following her.

Martha whirled around and looked up at the officer as if for protection. "Brick?"

"Martha was your late husband's sister, Mrs. Lord."

"Assuming she had a husband," the younger woman continued. "We don't know that for sure."

Brickman gave her an annoyed look but didn't say anything.

Sydney, however, was not so complacent. "What makes you doubt Kenneth was my husband?"

Arms crossed over her chest, Martha glared at her. "He wouldn't have gotten married without letting me know."

"Surprise. He did."

"Prove it."

"Martha, you're being particularly obnoxious, even for you," Benno stated as he drew alongside Sydney. The dark-haired woman gave him a furious look, but it didn't stop him. "Kenneth is dead and his widow is in mourning. I would think you might feel some grief for your own brother's death."

Her expression changed from confrontational to crushed so quickly that Sydney wondered if Martha was only doing what her audience expected her to.

"I can't believe Kenneth is dead," she said softly. "I can't believe any of this. When I spoke to him last Monday he didn't even mention he was involved with a woman."

Sydney shook her head. "You couldn't have seen your brother. He was with me."

"I spoke to him on the phone. I was visiting friends in Seattle. He said he was calling from the Portland office."

"Impossible." While Sydney knew Kenneth split his time and business between Portland and the Coast, he hadn't been away from her long enough to make the round trip, much less conduct business from his office. Besides which, she remembered Monday vividly. "That's the day Kenneth asked me to marry him in Lincoln City."

"Kenneth wasn't a liar," Martha insisted. "You're not even wearing a wedding ring. I'm still waiting for you to prove that you and Kenneth were married."

Sydney wasn't about to say anything about the ring, especially not after what had happened the night before. Wanting to give the other woman the benefit of the doubt, she told herself Martha was grief-stricken. Kenneth's sister had her days confused. Grief made people say and do odd things. She had to be more understanding than this.

As for giving the skeptical woman proof...

"Will a marriage license satisfy you?"

"It'll do for a start."

"Fine. I'll be right back."

Dignity keeping her back rigid, Sydney strode to the stairs and climbed them to her room, all the while trying to mentally place the whereabouts of the document. She remembered folding the license and slipping the paper into her purse after the justice of the peace had signed it. They hadn't had time to register the marriage that day...and then there had seemed no point to doing so.

When she didn't find the license in her purse, Sydney methodically searched her suitcases and then the drawers in the gilded dresser that she'd filled with her clothing and other personal items. After a few minutes she sensed she wasn't alone. She spun around to find Benno silently watching her from the doorway.

"Need some help?"

Her first instinct was to say no. But she'd gone through her own possessions. Only her late husband's were left, and she wasn't emotionally strong enough to go through them yet.

She nodded. "My brother Dakota took Kenneth's luggage to the master bedroom. Maybe the license is with his things."

A few minutes later, Sydney watched Benno do what she couldn't. While he kneeled among the suitcases and searched, she inspected the room. The clean lines of Scandinavian teak furniture contrasted with the fussy guest bedroom.

"Nothing," Benno finally said, sitting back on his haunches.

She met his gaze, pleading with her eyes as well as with her words. "Are you sure? Maybe you overlooked one of those inner pockets or something."

"Why don't you just admit you're a phony," Martha said from behind her. "Brick, arrest this woman immediately!"

Sydney turned to stare at Kenneth's sister who wasn't even willing to give her the benefit of the doubt.

Brickman asked, "Uh, on what grounds?"

"I don't know. Impersonation of someone who doesn't exist. Suspicion of foul play. You're the police, make something up!"

Sydney's sense of unreality was growing. This wasn't happening to her. Married and widowed in the same day... imagining Kenneth was still alive... and now this, not being able to prove her relationship to the man she'd married and having her arrest ordered by his sister. She could see Kenneth so clearly, just as if she had a picture of him in her mind.

A picture...

"That's it." Sydney raised her chin and told herself to hang in there a while longer. "The photographs!"

"What?" Martha demanded. "Another ploy?"

Sydney thought she understood the reason Kenneth hadn't told his sister about their plans. Perhaps he'd been afraid she'd spoil their wedding by trying to make them both miserable. Martha had been Kenneth's responsibility, but she wasn't Sydney's.

And Sydney wouldn't put up with the younger woman's spiteful behavior much longer. She'd thought she might make peace with her past and herself here in Kenneth's home, but she wouldn't succeed with Martha around to needle her. Right now, the thing Sydney desired most was to be out of Stone Beach!

"I shot a roll of film on our wedding day," she informed them all calmly. "I took several photographs of Kenneth—and we even posed together with the justice of the peace."

Martha was visibly disturbed by the information. Dark eyes wide, she took a step back. "Photographs? Where?"

"They're still in the camera." The tragedy had made Sydney forget not only about the film, but the camera as well. "I, uh, dropped it when Kenneth..."

The scene of his falling flashed in her mind and she had to take a deep breath.

"The camera should still be there where you left it, right?" Benno asked.

Sydney nodded. "On the rise, where I was taking the photos."

"Likely story." Martha sneered. "I'd predict that either you conveniently won't be able to find the camera—or the pictures will be ruined from exposure to the elements."

"There's one way to find out." Benno placed a palm square in the middle of Sydney's back, and with gentle pressure, moved her out of the room toward the stairs.

"Count me out," Martha stated. "I'm not traipsing around out on those rocks in high heels and a designer dress."

Sick of the woman's histrionics, Sydney couldn't help saying, "No one invited you."

"Brick! Do something!"

The woman continued ranting to the policeman as Sydney and Benno left the house. Her raised voice followed them down toward the cliff, but Sydney shut it out.

Retracing her steps brought back memories of her wedding day. Benno's presence kept her calm and focused on her mission. In fact, she would have broken down under Martha's onslaught if it hadn't been for his strength. He was so much more complex than she had guessed. Despite having started that ridiculous argument earlier, Benno seemed capable of giving her exactly what she needed at precisely the right moment.

As if he sensed Sydney's thoughts, Benno drew alongside and attempted to reassure her. "Don't let Martha get to you. She can be controlled."

"By you, maybe."

"By anyone who has starch enough to stand up to her." He swept a hand up her spine and gave her a friendly pat on the back. "You have a good backbone yourself. You just happen to be in a vulnerable position and she's taking advantage of that."

Sydney shook her head. "I can't imagine siblings being less alike. Kenneth was so sweet, so charming, so gallant."

"Kenneth?" Benno sounded surprised. "Hmm, that doesn't sound like him, either, but I guess you and I see him from different perspectives, being of the opposite sex. But you're right about Martha—a changeling if I ever met one."

He kept her distracted until they arrived at the scene of the accident. Within minutes, Sydney found the camera, which was barely dented. Thank goodness the housing was dry and the rewind mechanism was working properly. She opened the camera back and popped out the roll.

Greatly relieved, she held up her proof to show Benno. "Let Martha try to have me arrested after she sees these!"

Chapter Four

"You don't have to drive me to town," Sydney told Benno as she came downstairs to find him waiting for her.

She'd changed into a pair of loose white pants and a big blue cotton shirt fastened at the waist with a hand-tooled leather belt. The roll of film was secure inside the matching shoulder bag snuggled against her chest. She clung to the purse, afraid the final proof of her connection to Kenneth might disappear as mysteriously as her marriage license had.

"Driving you is no problem," Benno assured her.

He walked straight to the driveway, empty now save for his vehicle. Martha and Brickman had left, and her own car was parked in the garage. He opened the black Thunderbird's passenger door.

"Get in," he said, circling the sports car and sliding behind the wheel.

An order rather than a request, Sydney thought. Now that her head was clear and her anger burned brightly, she was capable of handling things. Benno DeMartino cared what happened to her. She didn't want to mention anything and put him off with some misplaced sense of pride.

Why did she feel so attached to a man who had been a stranger less than twenty-four hours ago? And why did he feel responsible for her?

"There are a couple of places that handle film, but Stone Beach Photos has the best service," Benno told her.

They locked gazes as he started the engine. Sydney felt both comforted and anxious. She couldn't explain her strange reaction. It was almost as if she was attracted to the man. Relieved when he broke their gaze and looked over his shoulder to back out of the driveway, she settled into the bucket seat.

"We'll get the questions about your marriage straightened out tomorrow," Benno said, swinging the car toward town. "Don't kid yourself about Martha's leaving town. Wherever she's off to, she'll be back. Think you can handle her alone tonight?"

"I'm tougher than I look."

Troubled by the unusual way she'd been acting, Sydney was determined to regain her strength. Normally she was a leader, efficiency in motion. But the last several months—especially the past few days—had taken the starch out of her. She hated feeling helpless. And beholden. Still, she didn't want Benno to think she wasn't grateful for his continued support, no doubt offered so generously because of his friendship with Kenneth.

"Listen," she said, "I appreciate your believing in me, especially since you don't even know me."

"Maybe I know you better than you think."

Sydney had long considered herself insightful when it came to reading people, but with her senses askew, she could no longer be sure of anything. Except

Benno, an inner voice added. Her instinct told her she could count on him.

Main Street was clean and neat and alive. People of all ages stared at display windows and entered the quaint-looking shops that lined the half-mile stretch.

"Lots of tourist activity today," Benno commented.

"Is that unusual? It is August."

"It's also a Wednesday. This place has always been a madhouse from Friday through Sunday, spring through fall, but weekdays used to be a lot slower."

"Maybe tourism is picking up."

"Being a businessman, I should hope so, but I preferred Stone Beach when it went at a slower pace. That's why I came back."

From where? Something kept Sydney from pursuing an answer. Later, she promised herself. Later she would get answers to a lot of questions that had sprung to mind.

After waiting for a family of vacationers to cross in the middle of the block, Benno pulled into a diagonal space in front of Stone Beach Photos. As he held the door open for her, the bell attached to it jingled. She preceded him inside, brushing his arm. An awareness washed through Sydney that troubled her.

"What can I do for you?" a red-headed man behind the counter asked.

Sydney dug into the shoulder bag. "I have some film that needs to be developed as soon as possible."

"It costs a little extra, but I can guarantee next-day service." The man gave her an envelope. "Fill this in."

The bell jingled, signaling the entrance of another customer, but beside her, Benno stiffened. Sydney looked up when she finished scribbling her name.

Parnell Anderson had entered the shop with Officer Mick Brickman right behind him.

"DeMartino," the auburn-haired man growled.

"Anderson."

It didn't take psychic powers to realize the two men didn't like each other. They squared off, each hostile and wary of the other, while, hands hooked in his gun belt, Brickman guarded the door. Amusement curled his thick lips. Sydney was instantly edgy. After she'd scrawled out her address, she dropped the roll of film into the envelope and handed the package to the clerk.

"What time can I pick up the photos?" she asked, wanting to get out of the shop as quickly as possible. The atmosphere was charged with hostility and she'd had enough of that.

"Make it after four in the afternoon to be safe."

"Great. I'll be here about that time tomorrow."

About to suggest they leave, Sydney was stopped by Anderson's challenge to Benno.

"I was amazed that you weren't at your buddy's memorial service."

"I was out of town. On business."

Anderson's eyes never left Benno's face. "Fate works in strange ways, doesn't it?"

"What the hell is that supposed to mean?"

"You and Lord returning to the scene of the crime... his drowning... perhaps a higher power was exacting justice, at last."

Bewildered by the statement, Sydney looked to Benno. His eyes were narrowed on the other man, his body stiff as if he were barely holding himself in check. Spontaneously, she placed a hand on his arm, and gazed at him steadily until she got his attention.

When he looked down at her, his expression was hard, but Sydney wasn't afraid.

"I'm finished here," she said quietly, ignoring the other men. "We can leave now."

The coldness in Benno's light brown eyes thawed. Nodding, he led the way out of the shop.

"So, what can I do for you, Cousin Parnell?" the clerk asked as the door closed behind them.

STILL TICKED OFF by his encounter with Parnell, Benno let Sydney take the lead.

"I could use a walk," she said, stopping near his car.

Not wanting to be alone yet, he asked, "Want some company?"

"I thought you had to open the coffeehouse."

"In a while."

"Come on, then." She headed west across the street. "The beach is public property."

Because her tone was warm and inviting, Benno didn't take offense. He was sure that Sydney was happy to have someone to talk to. As was he. Maybe she would keep his mind off Parnell's comment about a higher power exacting justice—and the guilt that had haunted him for almost twenty years.

Approaching the beach and the treacherous waters beyond, Benno knew he would never forget. Neither would Parnell. The past would forever lie between them like a closed coffin. Parnell had never made any bones about wanting revenge.

Revenge?

The word echoed through his mind.

Could it be? No. Impossible. Kenneth's death had been an accident, one Sydney had witnessed, Benno reminded himself. Parnell had merely been gloating.

"You and Parnell Anderson don't like each other much," Sydney stated as they reached the steps that led down to the beach.

"No."

She stopped long enough to kick off her sandals and gather them up by the straps before continuing down the steps and north along the hard-packed strip. People were scattered along the beach, some on blankets, others in the water. A handful of teenagers in colorful wetsuits were farther out, about to mount their sleek boards and surf their way out from the shallows.

"And he didn't like Kenneth, either," Sydney continued.

"No."

Her voice was controlled when she asked, "Then why did he show up at the memorial service?"

Benno didn't answer. How could he tell her Parnell had probably attended to offer a prayer of thanks.

"I knew something wasn't right," she went on. "I didn't sense any sorrow in him."

"Parnell Anderson likes to establish his importance whenever possible."

The eldest Anderson sibling had always thrown his weight around, ever since Benno could remember. Benno had been a gutsy kid, Parnell a spoiled teenager the first time they'd come nose-to-nose. Parnell had hated him for being tough—for not toadying to him the way Brickman always had—and still did.

"What crime?" Sydney asked, finally picking up on Parnell's accusation in the photo shop.

Caught off guard by Sydney's question, Benno found he had no quick, slick answer with which to put her off. She stopped short and he did the same. They stood so close he could have reached out and taken her in his arms, let her warmth and compassion comfort him the way his had comforted her. But she was his friend's widow, he reminded himself. He kept his hands at his sides. His fingers curled into fists.

"There was no official crime."

Even as Benno said it, guilt swept over him like the ocean breeze that ruffled Sydney's hair around her face. He stared into those fathomless eyes that seemed to plumb the depths of his soul. No, he hadn't been convicted of a crime, but that hadn't prevented his self-imposed punishment over the tragedy that he felt had been his fault. He'd left town in disgrace and had spent years not caring what happened to him—as if his self-destruction could have made up for what had happened.

"It's all right if you don't want to talk about it," Sydney told him, backing away. "But if you need a friendly ear..."

And he'd thought he was the one with the spare shoulder. He smiled at her. The answering glimmer from her eyes and mouth warmed him before she turned away and continued sauntering up the beach. She glanced over her shoulder and waited for Benno to join her. They were heading toward a formation of rocks that was strewn in the shallows. As always, Benno's gaze was drawn to The Sugar Loaf, the largest and most unusual of the group.

"I know what it's like to be different," she said, dodging a little boy who headed straight for them in a bright yellow beach trike.

Benno followed her example. Several kids were having a race in the low-slung, wide vehicles with oversize tires designed especially to careen along the hard-packed sand.

"Who said anything about being different?" he asked. "What are you? Psychic?"

Her silence forced Benno to study her unsmiling face more closely. She'd talked about hearing voices, about seeing her dead husband. He'd attributed her fanciful state to grief, but, unless he was mistaken, he'd hit on something—not that he necessarily believed her.

"My special talents weren't often appreciated by others," she admitted. "I was derided and disbelieved. Through painful experience, I learned to submerge part of myself so others could be comfortable around me." More softly, she added, "So I could be comfortable with myself."

"What kind of talents?" Benno joked. "Knowing when the phone is about to ring? Predicting who'll win the Superbowl?"

Her forehead wrinkled as she glanced at him. "I was hoping you might take me seriously."

Because he wasn't sure he could, and because he didn't want to admit that to her, he merely said, "I'm listening."

Sydney stood facing the sugar-loaf-shaped rock in the distance. She seemed to be trying to make up her mind whether or not she could trust him.

"Really," he added.

Slowly she turned and began to walk back the way they had come. "I—I sensed things, knew things other people didn't." Face turned away toward the sea, her voice was low and muffled by the surf and the sound of gulls wheeling overhead. "Sometimes dreams would tell me things. Other times I was awake when I saw the visions—mostly frightening ones."

"Like nightmares?"

Her expression solemn, she asked, "Do you ever dream?"

"Sure, doesn't everyone?"

"And do you understand what each dream means?"

Benno shrugged. "Not necessarily, but I can relate them to things that have happened to me."

"These dreams or visions, if you will were... different. They weren't necessarily about me and they were rarely about the past."

"Premonitions?"

She nodded. "I learned to hate them when I was eight years old, the first time the experience became more than a game. I saw my brother Dakota playing in an abandoned building. I knew he was in danger, that something terrible was going to happen to him. I didn't know what—I couldn't always take these things literally. Even so, I was scared. I told my father."

"And he didn't believe you."

"He didn't want to." A slight tremor overtook her fingers as she brushed the hair from her face. "I remember him yelling at me, shaking me, ordering me to stop making up stupid stories."

"And did this premonition come true?"

"Yes, a few days later. Dakota almost fell through the rotten floor to the basement, but his clothes caught on some jagged wood. One of his buddies was with him and got help. He was cut and bleeding. Twenty-seven stitches in his side. Three days in the hospital." Her eyes filled with pain as they met Benno's. "My father blamed me. He said Dakota would never have thought of going into that building if I hadn't put the idea into his head.''

"Kind of rough on an eight-year-old."

"Especially since I never told my brother about what I had seen." Her voice lowered to a whisper. "If he didn't know, how could I have made him do it?"

Even though Sydney denied her guilt, she seemed uncertain, as if she did blame herself, Benno thought. He placed an arm around her back and soothed her shoulder with a protective hand. He led her around a young couple sprawled out in the sand on a blanket, stereo blasting, dark glasses shading their eyes from the natural beauty around them.

Sydney didn't seem to notice them. She went on talking. "Age didn't matter. Knowing things other people didn't was always rough. A few years back, a wealthy friend of mine met a man at a local bar. Candace told me she was in love with him and that she was getting married. I never met Lex. But premonition, sixth sense…whatever you call it, made me believe the guy was a fortune hunter. And dangerous. I warned Candace."

"I take it she didn't appreciate your interference."

Sydney shrugged. "I should have kept my mouth shut. I'm not sure exactly what happened, but telling her led to a breakup of the proposed marriage, and it made our friendship pretty rocky for a while."

"Sometimes being a friend isn't the easiest thing for any of us," Benno said. He'd gained that knowledge firsthand.

"I was right about Lex. He was vindictive—to get even he stole some of Candace's jewelry. Eventually she and I got together again, though our relationship was never quite the same. Still, I hated the responsibility. Sick of it all, I made an effort to reject what I had come to think of as my curse. I tried to be like everyone else, and changing wasn't easy.''

Speaking from a totally different point of view, but one equally compelling, Benno said, ''It's difficult denying who we really are.'' Especially when certain people were determined not to let you forget.

''In the end, I had to see a hypnotherapist who helped me suppress the dreams and visions. I can't tell you how relieved I was when I finally believed I had succeeded. Now that disturbing part of myself seems to be reawakening.'' A sharp edge to her voice cut through Benno when she amended, ''Either that, or I'm going crazy.''

''I don't think you're crazy to love someone so much you wish them alive.''

If only that were possible....

Benno dropped his arm. There it was again. They were supposedly discussing Sydney's problems, but his memories kept haunting him. Maybe it was the place. He'd chosen to return to Stone Beach because he'd had something to prove to himself. Too bad he was making such a damn poor job of it.

They continued in silence until he realized they were approaching his beachhouse and farther up the street, his place of business. He checked his watch.

''Listen, I really do have to open up my place. If you're not in a hurry to get back—''

She jumped on the offer. ''If I wouldn't be in the way.''

''A potential customer is never in the way,'' he stated firmly, though there was more to his wanting

Sydney's continued company than her business. Her mere presence made him feel better about himself.

"All right. I'm not in any hurry to get ho...back."

Benno immediately registered that she'd chosen not to call the house on the cliff home. As they left the beach area, he wondered whether she would choose to stay or leave once Kenneth's estate was settled. He didn't know where she was from or where she was headed. He didn't really know much about her at all, Benno reminded himself.

"There seems to be someone waiting for you," she told him.

That someone was leaning against the front door, her arms crossed over her buxom chest, her pretty face serene as she watched them cross Main Street.

"It's about time, boss," the dark-haired woman called. "I thought you ditched this place, leaving me out of a job."

Benno smiled as he introduced her to Sydney. "This is Poppy Kehl, my only full-time employee—and the only one with a mouth that's going to get her into trouble one of these days."

"He believes in getting his money's worth," Poppy complained good-naturedly as she held out her hand. "Meet the combination cook, waitress and barmaid."

Sydney shook Poppy's hand. "I'm Sydney Raferty."

"Sydney Raferty?" the brunette echoed, flipping her long, glossy ponytail over her shoulder. "Aren't you the—"

"Kenneth Lord's widow," Sydney finished for her.

Unlocking the door, Benno noticed her smile fade, making him feel selfish and slightly guilty for wanting her company.

"Tough break. I was really sorry to hear about the accident," Poppy murmured. "I never really got to know Kenneth very well." Then the cheery disposition Benno was used to took over as she changed the subject. "So, did the boss hire you to give me some help?"

"I'm afraid not."

"I didn't think so." She followed Benno inside. "The man's a slave driver."

Benno gave the woman he'd known since grammar school days a sharp look as he crossed to the bar. "And if you had said yes, Sydney, Poppy here would be complaining about how her tips would be cut in half."

Poppy ignored that. "Someone's got to keep the man on his toes. With those looks, he could get away with anything, with practically anyone."

"Except Poppy," he clarified.

Not that he had ever been interested in her in that way. Though they'd both lived on the shanty side of town as youths, they'd been too smart to get hooked up with each other. When he'd returned to Stone Beach a few months back, they'd picked up their friendship as if he hadn't been gone for all those years.

"I like a man who's more romantic," Poppy said with a smirk.

"She means manageable." Benno didn't add that Poppy had been through half the available men in town including her three ex-husbands, the first of whom had been Mick Brickman. He never had figured out the attraction there.

Poppy took a white apron from a hook and put it around her fully rounded hips, which were encased in a pair of too-tight jeans. "I appreciate a man who's not afraid of a woman with a mind of her own."

Sydney laughed. "So do I."

"We'll get along just fine then. Where are you from?"

"Seattle originally. But I've been living and working in L.A. since college."

Upending the bar stools, Benno was surprised by the information. She didn't seem the type.

"Working in the movie business?" Poppy asked as she went behind the bar and started setting up cups next to the espresso-cappuccino maker.

"Advertising," said Sydney, sliding onto a stool. "I was a creative director with Long and Betz Creative Resources. Bite Brite Toothpaste . . . Scribble Pens . . . Surf'n'Tan . . . those were some of my accounts. I quit last month."

Realizing the two women were hitting it off, Benno was glad he'd brought Sydney along. Relaxed as she was now, she seemed like a different person than the woman who'd raised his protective instincts. Different, and infinitely more appealing.

He wondered about the real woman. How much stock could he put in this psychic business? Although skeptical, he didn't rule out Sydney's "visions." He would like to believe everything she'd told him—but he remembered the tarot cards spread out on the coffee table. He would be sorely disappointed to find out she was yet another New Age fad believer. He'd met enough of them in the years he'd spent in tinseltown.

In any case, why should it matter to him?

Being completely honest with himself, Benno admitted he was attracted to his friend's widow—no matter how inappropriate that might seem.

EVERYTHING WAS GOING according to plan.

That was the thought uppermost in his mind as he kissed Martha Lord passionately. Through the kiss, he smiled at her naïveté. She clung to him with the desperation of a woman in love. She believed in him.

She would do anything for him.

And he would do anything... for himself.

His smile widened as he set the dark-haired witch from him just far enough to plant a slash of annoyance in her eyes. He knew just how to work her, how to get what he wanted. He cupped her shoulders and stroked the tension out of them with seductive fingers.

"So what are you going to do now?" he asked as if his only motive was to support her.

"I'm going to move in, of course."

He laughed. "Your Sydney will be pleased."

Martha's dark eyes narrowed unflatteringly. One day he would have the pleasure of telling her how truly unattractive he sometimes found her. But not today.

"She's not *my* Sydney and I don't care what that tramp thinks," Martha said, her mouth setting in a pout. "That's my house now that Kenneth is dead. Everything is mine."

"And soon it will be ours," he murmured, kissing her again.

Little did Martha know that he had more of an interest in Sydney than she did. Little did she know that she was playing right into his hands. When Martha melted against him in complete surrender, he freed her lips.

"Unless you've changed your mind. Perhaps you'll be bored with me once you have your hands on all that money."

"Bored? Never. We'll find new ways to keep ourselves amused with Kenneth's money." An expression of doubt crossed her narrow face. "The photographs—they could ruin everything. If that tramp—"

"Shh." He put a finger to her lips. "Don't even think it. Nothing is going to be ruined. Not as long as we're together."

He'd taken care of the photographs just as he had the marriage certificate. He would have it all . . . and Sydney Raferty would rue the day she'd crossed him.

WHEN SHE FINALLY tore herself away from Benno's Place, Sydney realized how drawn she was to its proprietor. His hard good looks were difficult to ignore, as Poppy had pointed out. And more than that, she recognized within him a kindness and generosity of spirit that few people she was acquainted with possessed.

Best of all, he made her feel.

And yet, the knowledge that Benno lit a spark of life within her made Sydney as edgy and troubled as had their conversation on the beach. What in the world was she thinking of to be so interested in another man when her husband was just buried?

If he were indeed dead—she couldn't quite suppress the notion that Kenneth might be alive.

Mind churning, Sydney wished she could trust her so-called gifts, even though she'd gone to such lengths to rid herself of them. Too much had happened in the last weeks to ignore. The dreams, the visions....

How could she know what to believe when she'd been under so much stress that she'd walked away from a career it had taken her ten years to build?

There were times when she could barely tell reality from fantasy. Like last night when she'd imagined she'd found her wedding ring on the nightstand. She was tired, and not only in body but in spirit. So tired.

Closing her eyes, Sydney stopped for a moment and concentrated on the events of the night before. The ring. The fuzzy memory crystallized. She could feel the gold's weight, the rough outer texture, the engraving on the inside circle of the band. That had all been real, hadn't it? Thinking hard, she remembered clasping the symbol of her marriage in her palm. Then Benno had come up behind her on the deck. He had startled her. She'd lost her balance, and the ring had gone flying....

If the ring had, indeed, existed.

Eyes opening, Sydney suddenly realized she was standing in front of the house, in the middle of the empty driveway. Martha hadn't returned. She was alone on the property. Why not check for herself, see if she could find the ring?

Wandering around to the back of the house, she stopped below her balcony in a shady area nearly free of grass. The sun was setting, its thin beams squeezing through the stand of trees behind her. But since there was enough daylight, she could still see clearly, and if she had really dropped the ring in the area, she would find it.

After gauging the trajectory a small object might take were it to fly from the balcony, she backed up a few yards. While the day's warmth had hardened the earth, the soil was still damp from days of rain. On the ground were a man's footprints...and a couple of cigarette stubs. She bent to pick one up and her heart began to pound. Thin and dark brown, this was the type of cigarette Kenneth smoked.

Nothing unusual about finding them on his own property, she told herself.

Reminded of her short-lived marriage, Sydney squeezed her eyes tight against the threat of tears. Once she got herself under control, she continued her search halfheartedly. More footprints led off into a wooded area, punctuated by another cigarette butt on the trail.

She returned to the original spot and stared up at the perfect view of the balcony and windowed doors. What fascination had Kenneth had with the guest bedroom?

Sydney rubbed her arms as a chill shot through her and her head went light, a forewarning. She stopped as a last ray of light beamed through the trees to fall at her feet. Her gaze followed the ray to its end where a glimmer caught her eye.

The ring?

Sydney bent to retrieve the object but was disappointed when she rose with it in her hand.

Not a ring, but a coin.

An arcade token, she corrected as she inspected the round metal piece more carefully. The imprint was distinctive. A seagull in flight on one side, a boardwalk on the other.

What in the world would an arcade coin be doing on the property?

Chapter Five

No sooner had the question occurred to her than Sydney heard a car pull up into the driveway. Slipping the token into an outside pocket of her shoulder bag, she rounded the house to see who had arrived.

Martha's white Porsche stood in the driveway and the woman herself was pulling a large suitcase from the trunk. She'd changed from the red silk sundress to a gold lamé jumpsuit with giant beaded shoulders and a plunging neckline. Dressed so elaborately, Martha must have had special plans for the evening. Good. Then Sydney could spend the time alone. Unfortunately, peace of mind was not to be hers yet.

"Planning on staying long?" she asked, trying to keep her voice friendly.

Martha gave her a haughty, knowing look. "You'd like me to leave, wouldn't you? So you could get hold of Kenneth's assets without a struggle?"

"I don't want to fight. I don't want—"

"Well, I could care less what you want. You have a fight on your hands, you little gold digger, whether or not you're ready for one."

Sydney gaped as Martha pushed by, almost hitting her with the suitcase. She stood staring at the rude woman. She'd been about to admit she didn't want anything of Kenneth's but a sentimental keepsake, a reminder of the love they'd shared, but now she'd bite her tongue before saying so. Martha Lord would merely laugh and deride her.

"Oh, by the way," Martha said, "I've already moved your things out of *my* bedroom."

"Your bedroom?"

"The one you've been using without my permission." Martha set down the suitcase in front of the door that she quickly unlocked. "I personally chose every object in that room." She threw open the door so that it strained against its hinges. "I'm not about to give them over to some upstart, no matter how short a time you intend to stay here."

Having already met Kenneth's sister, Sydney figured she should have guessed why the bedroom had seemed so repugnant. The decor was every bit as offensive as the woman who had chosen it.

"I put your things where they belong," Martha went on, "if you really are Kenneth's wife, that is." She entered the house and marched straight for the stairs. "I shudder to think the master bedroom was being defiled by a liar and a cheat."

Uneasy at the thought of staying in the room she'd been trying to avoid, Sydney swallowed her objections. Besides, now that she had met Martha, she had no desire to remain in the other woman's bedroom.

Crossing to the bottom of the staircase, she looked up at her sister-in-law. "All your doubts about my marriage to your brother will be put to rest tomorrow when I pick up the photographs from Stone Beach Photos."

On the landing, Martha paused, and her deep-set, dark eyes narrowed. "That's to be seen, isn't it? But no matter what you show me, my doubts will never be erased." Managing to sound genuinely upset, she added, "If you really did trick Kenneth into marrying you, you used some clever subterfuge or he wouldn't have excluded me from his plans."

With that, Martha disappeared into her room and slammed the door behind her.

Sydney breathed a sigh of relief and wondered if she could successfully avoid any more unpleasantness. She hoped her sister-in-law did have other plans for the evening so she would be free to roam the house at will. She dreaded entering the room she was to have shared with Kenneth; she couldn't tolerate the thought of being cooped up in there.

Deciding to take advantage of Martha's absence, Sydney found the dinner Asia had left her the day before and heated it in the microwave. By the time she'd eaten, darkness had fallen, and her sister-in-law emerged from her room. Although prepared for a confrontation, Sydney was thankfully spared. Without a word to her, Martha flounced out of the house and drove away in her Porsche.

Sydney checked all the first-floor doors and windows to make sure they were locked before returning to the kitchen where she intended to warm her milk. Not that she needed it tonight—she was exhausted and could barely keep her eyes open—but she didn't want to take any chances.

The refrigerator held a surprise, however. No milk carton. And she couldn't remember having seen it when she took out her food earlier. Maybe Benno had finished the milk that morning while he was making breakfast. No big deal, she assured herself as she turned off all the lights except the closest to the front door.

Finally, she ascended the stairs to Kenneth's bedroom.

Her heart pounded as she opened the door and she entered with a sense of trepidation. But she didn't sense any trace of Kenneth's presence.

How odd.

Putting away her things that Martha had strewn around the room gave her something upon which to concentrate. For a while, at least, she would have to dwell on what her first night in this room should have been like.

Too much time to think—that was her problem.

Thoughts too disturbing, too sad, too frightening.

Once finished organizing her belongings, she climbed into her comfortably familiar cotton nightdress and turned off all but a low light atop the chest of drawers. Then she curled up in a leather chair set at an angle near the windows. She rested her achy legs on a matching hassock. All the while she'd worked in the room, she'd been mentally preparing herself for this moment when she would have nothing to think about but Kenneth.

Yet as she looked through the glass doors out over the windswept grounds, the image Sydney confronted in her mind's eye was a strong, angular face framed by dark hair sliced back into a ponytail. The diamond in his ear winked, hypnotizing her until she drifted off to a place without fear....

DANGER WOUND ITS DARK PATH through the stand of trees. The runner fled, legs pounding the uneven ground, arms flailing against the black night, breath sucking at the humid air. Effort added onto effort, but to no avail. The runner seemed to be getting nowhere. The shelter of the trees was as good a place as any to stop, to control the choking spurt of fear.

Stealth and cunning meant safety.

The nearby ocean whispered its warning: *Be like a wild animal—seek cover. Camouflage. A hiding place. Otherwise, be recaptured, caged . . . and then what?*

The crunch of dried branch underfoot warned of another presence.

Heart pounding . . . pulse ringing . . . gut churning. . . .

It's now or never—must run!

Too late.

Confronted, the hunted lunged for the hunter and forced away the hand with the gun. But, with seeming ease, the deadly weapon revolved inexorably inward.

Heart nearly rupturing from fright, the would-be victim cried out. No sound. The barrel lined up in slow motion, its perfect round mouth a dark, yawning chasm of death.

Use both hands to stop it! the ocean warned.

No grip.

Something pulling free. . . .

Curled fingers securing the object, the victim was pushed backward from the force of a bullet. The ground hit hard, ungiving. A gush of salty blood welled and gurgled past dry, cracked lips while disbelieving eyes widened with shock.

"Why?"

The single rasp was swallowed by an explosion.

"Aaahhh!" The gunshot still ringing in her head, Sydney screamed herself awake.

Body rigid, the fingers of her right hand clutched in a painful fist, she looked down at her stomach that was pulsating with pain and frantically patted the front of her white nightgown. Except for the clinging dampness caused by her sweat, the garment was clean—free of the brilliant red she had seen so clearly in the dream. She took a choked breath and opened her clenched fingers. Though the flesh felt penetrated, her palm was empty.

"A dream," she choked out.

But the fear and the noise and the pain had all been so real!

Sydney quickly looked around the room to make sure she was still safe. Nothing out of line. The light on the chest of drawers shone. The door was closed. The windows were locked. Yet she was shaking as if the earth had quaked beneath her. This dream had been even more violent than any previous ones.

Heart wildly palpitating, Sydney tried to calm herself and replay the nightmare in her mind while it was still possible to remember.

She was running—no, a man—no, she.

Which?

Think harder.

A dark-haired man, she decided, closing her eyes. She grasped the image and refused to let go. A dark-haired man was running from someone. Terrified. Determined. But who? She couldn't make out his features. Too murky. Even so, his fear became her own. Terror welled within her anew, cradled her in its ugly grasp, threatened to swallow her whole.

And then the foreboding receded and dissipated altogether.

She squeezed her eyelids shut tighter. "No, not yet."

Unable to retain the vision any longer, Sydney opened her eyes and gasped in frustration.

How should she interpret what she had seen? Was someone in danger? A dark-haired man?

Kenneth had dark hair, but he was already dead, wasn't he?

Her thoughts turned to the only other dark-haired man in her life. Benno DeMartino. But he was definitely alive. At least for now, a nasty little voice whispered.

She sprang out of the chair and reached for the telephone on the nightstand. Probably sounding like a madwoman, she demanded the number of Benno's Place from the operator. Then, with shaky fingers, she punched out his number. Four rings.

"Benno's Place," came a woman's voice over the blare of a jukebox and noisy customers in the background.

"Poppy? It's Sydney. Can I speak to Benno?"

"He's not here."

"Not there?" Anxiety made Sydney's pulse pound. She hadn't considered that she might not be able to warn him. What if he was in danger at this very moment? "Where is he?"

"I haven't the faintest idea. He left a half hour or so ago and told me he'd be back in a while..." Poppy's voice trailed off as someone shouted to her. Then she said, "Listen, I'm the only one here and the natives are getting restless. I've got to go. Should I give Benno a message?"

"Tell him to call me."

Sydney set the receiver in its cradle and checked the bedside clock. 12:26 a.m. Where could Benno be so late? Surely nothing had happened to him yet.

Suddenly, she realized where she was. She was sitting on the bed. Kenneth's bed. And she was feeling nothing but concern for a man other than her late husband. Unable to conjure up even a little guilt, she propped up the pillows behind her and waited. With the passing of each minute, her anxiety lessened and her doubts about the dream increased.

The clock read 12:39 before the telephone rang. Sydney snatched the receiver.

"Is something wrong?" came Benno's concerned voice.

She let out a shaky breath. "I don't know...I mean, no, not with me, not now."

"What? Did someone try to break into the place?"

She was confused until she remembered the incident with the lights the other night. "No. It was one of those awful dreams I told you about."

A moment of silence was followed by his offering, "You want me to come up there?"

"It's okay. I don't need you to hold my hand," she told him. Though she might not mind his doing so, she thought with a sense of shock that she was being disloyal to Kenneth. "I wanted you to know..."

Now she was feeling a little foolish.

"Know what?"

"Be careful. Someone may be planning to hurt—"

"Wait a minute, would you?"

Despite her growing reservations, Sydney would have explained further if Benno hadn't interrupted. She heard his interchange with a couple of customers, one of whom sounded as if he was getting out of line.

Then she heard the downstairs door open and close and the clack of heels tap against the wooden floor. Martha. She must just be coming in now. Sydney held her breath as her sister-in-law ascended the stairs and then passed her door.

Benno was talking to her again. "Listen, I have a nasty situation here." His tone was terse. "Can I call you back?"

Now Sydney was really feeling impulsive. She had no concrete reason to believe Benno was in danger. And, if he were, the situation wasn't necessarily imminent. The explanation could definitely be put off, she decided, if not forgotten.

"No, don't call me back," she finally said. "This discussion can wait."

"Why don't I pick you up for a late lunch tomorrow afternoon," he suggested. "Say 1:30? You can tell me all about your dream then, before we go over to Stone Beach Photos to pick up the pictures."

Relief shot through her, warming her. Sydney thought she'd be performing that task alone. But Benno wasn't planning to abandon her in the middle of the crisis.

"All right," she agreed. "1:30 tomorrow afternoon."

Sydney hung up and leaned back against the pillows. Though she was by no means at ease with the dream and its implications, most of her anxiety had subsided. She'd gone through too many years of this experience not to recognize it for what it was: a warning.

Whether or not she wanted to be in tune with her most basic self, she didn't seem to have a choice. Therefore, she had to act on what she knew, and with knowledge came responsibility. Her whole world seemed determined to turn upside down, and it was up to her to right it again.

"I CAN'T BE SURE who is in danger—you, me, or someone else entirely," Sydney was saying over lunch at The Sugar Bowl, a restaurant at the north end of town.

"Dreaming about death isn't so unusual under the circumstances." Benno glanced out the window across the beach to The Sugar Loaf, the largest of a dozen seastacks dotting the shallows—the one that reminded him of death every time he saw it. "Nor is the fact that you dreamed about a man."

"I can see your point, but I hope you can see mine."

He'd been listening with a combination of alarm and disbelief. "What? That I should take this warning seriously?"

"Yes!" she said, the single word ringing with frustration. "A few weeks ago, I dreamed I was drowning—"

"Not to mention being caught up in myriad other dangers," Benno quickly reminded her. Picking up the second half of his grilled chicken sandwich, he noticed she hadn't eaten a thing. "You really ought to try something. The food here is great."

She ignored the suggestion. "But *I* wasn't the one who drowned."

"And you won't be the one shot."

She nodded. "That's entirely possible. You think I'm crazy, don't you."

"Only in the nicest of ways. Remember the premonition you had about your brother—you were sure he was the one in trouble. Why the doubts now?"

"Maybe I used to be more certain because I was more open then. Maybe if I'd been encouraged to work with professionals and develop my potential, I could give you all the answers. But I wasn't, and God knows I can only give you more questions."

Sydney's face was pale beneath her California tan. In the strong light of day, the freckles on her snub nose stood out, giving her a childlike innocence that belied the grown-up hell she was going through. Tension oozed from her and Benno knew she believed every word she was saying.

"This ability has made me nothing but unhappy and that's the reason I've suppressed it for so long," she went on. "But the dream invaded my peace whether or not I wanted it, and I just can't let it go at that. Not after what happened to Kenneth. Do you understand?"

"I truly don't know what to say."

"Say you believe me at least on some level. Promise you'll be extra careful. When I tried to figure out who the dark-haired man could be—"

"You thought of me," Benno concluded. "Can't say I'm flattered."

Although perhaps he should be, considering she'd thought of him at all. Despite his own common sense, his attraction to Sydney was growing. And the fact that she cared enough to be worried about him made it even more difficult to remember that Sydney was the widow of his friend. But she was going through a tough time—he couldn't take advantage of her trust.

"At least try one of these curly fries," he insisted, to take his mind off temptation. "They're rolled in spices and fried in peanut oil."

"Try to take this seriously."

Caught by the urgency in her eyes, Benno was chilled. A connection sparked between them like a live current and he could feel the depth of her anxiety. He couldn't look away. She genuinely believed he was in danger—and how was he to know she wasn't wrong. He had enemies. Or rather one very powerful enemy who had intimated fate had worked its justice on Kenneth.

Fate or Parnell Anderson?

Kenneth's death had been an accident, one Sydney had witnessed.

Uncomfortable, Benno tore his gaze away from Sydney and signaled their waitress. "More coffee?" he said.

The woman nodded and went to get the pot.

"Well?" Sydney asked, obviously still waiting for an answer.

"I'll be careful."

Her lids lowered and she took a shaky breath. "Thank goodness."

"Now are you going to eat or what?"

Sydney chowed down as if she were starving. Indeed, she could use a couple of extra pounds to fill out the hollows, Benno thought. She looked delicate, vulnerable at times, but he'd felt flickers of her iron will more than once in the past two days. She was merely in a bad situation, one that could only get better once they'd picked up those photographs. He checked his watch as the waitress refilled his cup. Quarter after three. Less than an hour to go.

Benno kept Sydney busy talking about her advertising career until it was time to leave. She seemed grateful for the switch to a safer topic.

But a few minutes before four, as they walked the several blocks to Stone Beach Photos, he felt her tension return.

"I'll be glad when this is over," Sydney said. "Then Martha will get off my back."

"Don't count on it."

"Has she always been so unlikable?"

"Around me she has."

"I guess she was different with Kenneth."

"She usually knew how to wrap him around her little finger," Benno admitted. "Sometimes, her true colors slipped through the cracks, but Kenneth was always too easy on her. He felt guilty that he'd had his parents until he'd grown up but she was deprived of a real family at an early age."

"And so he took over."

"And made excuses for her. And kept control of her trust fund." Benno spotted the white Porsche before Sydney did. "Speaking of the devil, you have an audience for the unveiling."

Outside the photo shop, Martha was leaning back against her car door and Brickman was pressed close enough to her to dance, Benno thought. Now what was going on between those two? Brickman was as far away from Martha's type as a man could get. Could she be playing him to her own advantage?

"Isn't this a coincidence, running into you here?" Benno said as they approached the Porsche.

"Yes, isn't it?" Martha replied, not even trying to hide her contempt for them. She flicked her eyes away as if looking at them would contaminate her. "I was just telling Brick how I needed to buy some film, wasn't I?"

Brickman laughed softly. "Right."

"I didn't realize you were smart enough to use a camera."

With that, Benno swept Sydney past the couple, but he could feel them fast on his heels. Luckily, the store itself was empty and they wouldn't have to listen to Martha's poison tongue for too long.

As they crossed to the counter, Donald looked up from where he was setting out new stock. "I'll get your order right away." He walked over to the small bin that held several packets and pulled Sydney's free.

Her hands were shaky as she opened the envelope and pulled out the photos. Benno inserted himself as a barrier between her and Martha who anxiously waited a few yards away, Brickman at her side. Sydney's forehead creased as she looked at one photo, then the next. She held them out to show Donald.

"These aren't mine."

The clerk picked up the envelope and checked the written information. "It's your roll. Take a gander. Here's your name—right?"

"But the photographs aren't of anything I shot." She gave Benno a pleading look.

He took the stack from her and quickly shuffled through them. Tourist pictures of the Stone Beach area—but no shots of Kenneth or Sydney.

"I told you she was an impostor," Martha said, her voice rising to a hysterical note.

Sydney pleaded, "Maybe the rolls were mixed up at the lab."

"This is your name, isn't it?" Donald argued.

"That doesn't mean the wrong pictures couldn't have been put into my envelope."

"Brick, arrest this impostor." Martha's frenzy was now augmented by a choked sound that made it appear she was close to tears. "You have all the proof you need."

"Do you have orders that came in the same shipment?" Benno asked Donald.

The clerk quickly checked a list attached to the bin. "Nine came in this afternoon. Only three others left for pickup."

"Let's open them and see what we find," Benno suggested.

But checking proved fruitless. Sydney did not find a single photo she recognized.

"And if my other customers got the wrong order, I would have heard by now."

"Unless they didn't take the time to look yet," Sydney said optimistically.

Benno placed a hand on her shoulder. "If there was a mix-up at the lab, the photos might even have been switched with those from another store."

The theory was unlikely, but he didn't know what else to believe.

"I'll call the lab," Donald said. "I'm sure we'll hear by tomorrow if there's anything to your theory."

"No!" Martha shouted. "Tomorrow's too late. Brick, arrest her now."

"I can wait until tomorrow." Brickman rushed Martha off, softly saying, "And anyway, I need more than missing photos with which to build a case. I can't go on your word alone. I have to find proof of malfeasance."

As they left the store, Martha gave him a look half-pleading, half-searing and wheedled, "I have the utmost faith in you, Brick."

Benno wished he could say the same for Sydney. He wanted to be on her side if for no other reason than to oppose Martha. But now he couldn't help entertaining some doubts of his own. Sydney had come up with no proof of being Kenneth's wife.

How could he be sure any part of her story was true? No one else saw Kenneth Lord fall and no one found his body.

Benno added together all the strange things that had happened along with those that Sydney had told him about since he'd met her. She'd heard Kenneth's voice on the foggy beach. She'd claimed to have found and then lost a wedding ring she'd thrown out to sea at the memorial service. And she'd almost been the victim of yet another mysterious accident when he'd found her out on the deck. Kenneth supposedly had come to her then. Benno had sworn she was confused, her thoughts clouded by some kind of tranquilizer, but she had denied taking anything.

Now she was adamant about that damned dream. Would disaster befall him next? And if so, would Sydney herself be the one to bring about a second tragedy?

Benno studied her forlorn, slightly panicky expression. Her body was rigid as if she was barely holding herself together. He didn't think she was playacting. He was certain she believed everything she had told him—about Kenneth, about herself, about the premonitions. But the pieces weren't falling together.

So what in the hell was going on?

Only one explanation came to mind, Benno thought sadly.

If Sydney believed what she had been telling, perhaps she was losing her grip on reality.

THE STRAIN WAS GETTING to her.

Standing on the deck outside the living area, Sydney stared out over the property as the sun set on the horizon. Kenneth Lord's property. Kenneth, her late husband, she told herself vehemently. Not that she could prove it.

She didn't need a vision to know the lab wouldn't find her photos. What could have happened to them?

Even Benno doubted her. He hadn't said as much—he'd been very kind when he'd driven her home—but she had recognized his shift in attitude. Wary. And how could she blame him? She was beginning to doubt herself. Perhaps the stress had finally made her crack.

She was relieved Martha wasn't around to worsen the situation. All was quiet, at least temporarily.

As if having to convince herself that she hadn't imagined it all, she went over the past weeks since she'd left L.A. Since Kenneth had come into her life.

She replayed their every meeting, recounted their every conversation. She couldn't recall such detail if it hadn't actually happened to her, she assured herself. She remembered Kenneth's exact words when he proposed, his vows to love and cherish her when they married, his expression of disbelief when he knew he was about to die.

Sydney....

Startled by her whispered name, Sydney froze. An eerie sensation glided through her and for an instant, she felt light-headed. It was as if she and Kenneth were together again...suspended, floating, bathed by the mist of the ocean.

Sydney blinked and focused on her surroundings. Without realizing what she'd been doing, she had left the safety of the house. As if the siren wind had lured her to the scene of tragedy, she was standing on the cliff, at the very same spot where Kenneth had disappeared.

Wind whipped through her hair and clothes, urging her ever closer to the precipice.

Sydney, my love....

The rhythmic swell of the ocean called to her, its sharp salt scent assailing her nose. It was the ocean she heard, wasn't it? Not Kenneth. Her breath caught in her throat, she cocked her head and listened to its mesmerizing surge.

The sea was forever, she thought.

Water rushed stone, the undercutting process continuing to carve out chunks of nature's history as it had for centuries. The tide was coming in, its inexorable pull strong, enticing. Knowing she could solve all her problems in one grand gesture, she closed her eyes. And as on the day of the memorial service when she had first had the vision, Kenneth waited for her, his arms outstretched.

She could almost see him now...almost touch him.

"Sydney, my love, come to me...."

His voice or her own mind playing tricks on her?

Her eyes flew open and panic welled in her breast. She flipped around, lunged away from the edge, and in doing so, twisted her ankle. Pebbles skidded underfoot. She felt herself slipping, falling off balance—and for a brief moment she thought of how easy it would be to let nature take her, too.

"No!"

She caught herself and recoiled from the edge of the cliff. She wasn't crazy. She wasn't!

What other explanation was there? an insidious voice asked her.

"I don't know. I don't know!" she screamed into the ungiving wind.

But she wasn't ready to take the coward's way out!

Sydney moved up and away from the scene of the accident toward the stand of trees where she'd shot the film. Although the light was fading fast and she didn't really expect to find anything, compulsion drove her onward. The site was free of human reminder, not surprising since the winds assaulted the area so fiercely.

Her gaze swept every direction. Suddenly a chill shot through her and her head went light. Surely not now, she thought—she couldn't be losing it now. Forcing herself to maintain control, she sought the quickest way home. A shortcut crested the rise and would cut through the stand of trees sheltering the house.

Without hesitation, Sydney took off in that direction. Light had faded and the landscape was alive with shadows of all sizes. Round boulders, tall trees. She forced her mind to concentrate on the myriad dark shapes. She wound down through the small forested area. The light of the house shone through the trees. She accelerated, almost running along the rough trail.

A sense of unreality filled her. Shapes became grotesque. Sounds magnified. Every movement became an effort. Her foot met something unyielding. Rigid. Her upper body floated ahead, out of control. She put her hands out as the ground rushed up to meet her.

"Damn!" she cursed as she jolted to a teeth-jarring stop.

Sydney shook her head to clear it and pushed herself onto her hands and knees, but kept fighting the bulk that held her fast. She didn't want to look. Didn't want to know.

When she could deny it no longer, she acknowledged the impediment for what it was: a very stiff, very cold, very dead body.

Chapter Six

Three sets of lights bobbed and wavered as they ascended the hill like banners of a tag team making its way to the house. Three sets of lights; three cars. Sydney had called only the authorities—and Benno.

The hooded fleece sweatshirt she'd pulled on hadn't chased away the chill that had invaded her body and spirit. Perhaps Benno could. She didn't understand why he affected her so deeply. It wasn't her nature to be feckless, to hop from one man to the next. She only knew he made her feel safe.

In the woods, a dead man awaited them.

She was still shaking, her teeth were still chattering; she wrapped her arms around herself as the cars pulled up the driveway.

Benno was the first to emerge from his vehicle. She rushed to him as Officer Mick Brickman followed right behind. He would be the one to show, she thought dispiritedly, even though he hadn't taken the call. His hostile attitude was all she needed right now. And last—as she should have expected—was Martha. How could things be worse?

Then Benno's broad shoulders blocked her view as they surrounded her. Letting out a sigh of relief, Sydney touched her forehead to his beard-stubbled chin. She needed his support. She needed him.

"Are you okay?"

"Now I am." With Benno there, everything would be all right and she would be fine. "Thanks for coming." After the photo fiasco, she hadn't been certain he would take anything she said seriously.

"So where's this corpse?" Brickman demanded.

For once, Martha said nothing, merely hung behind the officer and waited.

For what? And why did she seem so nervous?

Sydney pointed to the copse southwest of the house. "Over there."

"What are we waiting for?" Brickman asked, flicking on his flashlight as he strode off.

Martha moved more quickly than Sydney thought possible for a woman in a too-tight skirt and high, backless heels. "Wait for me, Brick," she demanded, giving Sydney a sly look as she minced past. She caught the officer by his upper arm and played the helpless female. "A horrible killer might be lurking in the woods."

"Not unless he's returned to the scene of the crime," Sydney stated calmly. "The body was already stiff."

Martha made a choking sound and moved closer to the policeman's side. Brickman stopped, and with his flashlight, signaled Sydney to take the lead. Benno stayed right beside her, lending her his strength.

"You sure you don't have any idea who the victim could be?" he asked.

"Not a clue. I told you I didn't know anyone in this town." Sydney hesitated, then softly added, "He had to have been the man from my dream."

Benno didn't say anything, but the muscles of the arm that brushed hers tightened. The forested area loomed closer. She was desperate for him to believe her.

"I assumed the dark-haired man was you because I knew you, not because I saw an identifiable face," she went on. "I told you it was all confused, that one minute I was the hunted, the next it was a dark-haired man." Remembering the dried blood on the victim's shirtfront, she swallowed hard. "He was shot twice, once in the stomach, once in the chest, exactly as I dreamed it."

"What's that?" Martha asked. "You dreamed this man was murdered and then it actually happened?"

"Something like that," Sydney mumbled, hurrying on.

"Bri-i-ick." Martha whispered loudly enough for Sydney to hear. "I don't think she's all there, you know what I mean?"

Officer Brickman merely grunted.

Sydney wished she hadn't said anything, not until later when she could have discussed the situation with Benno alone, but how was she to know Martha had the ears of a cat? She supposed she should have guessed.

As the gap closed between them and the corpse's resting place, Sydney slowed, felt her feet grow heavy. Her stomach rumbled. Heaven knew there was nothing left to throw up, but she was being threatened by nausea once more. She took a deep breath and kept going, wielding the flashlight she'd brought from the house in an arc until the beam caught a glimmer of pale material. The man's shirt.

Still several yards away, she stopped cold and pointed the beam. "There."

Brickman and Martha swung by. Benno gave her an intense look before going after them. She couldn't stand over the victim just yet. Actually, she wished she never had to see the dead man again. And yet his ordinary face frozen in a grimace of fear or pain would be forever burned into her memory.

"Eeehh!"

Sydney jumped at Martha's scream.

"What the hell?" came Benno's voice.

"Good God!" Brickman said at the same time.

Sydney's stomach was tied in knots as she slowly approached the others. They were all three staring at her as if she had sprouted horns and a tail. Even Benno. Sydney's heart beat wildly as she realized how deeply disturbed he was, and not just at seeing a dead man.

"You recognize him?" she asked. That had to be the reason his expression was a combination of horror and sorrow.

"This is it, Brick. You can't ignore what's in front of your eyes. This was no accident. Kenneth was murdered. Now you have to arrest her." Abruptly Martha flew at Sydney, fingers with nails like claws leading. "Murderess!"

Sydney jumped away as Brickman grabbed Martha's arm, stopping her from following.

"What? I didn't—"

"Don't deny it. You killed my brother!"

Confused, filled with a growing feeling of horror, Sydney looked at Benno, who was strangely silent, his features twisted into an expression of sheer grief. Her heart beat wildly in her chest and she squeezed the flashlight so tightly her fingers went numb.

Brickman said, "Don't tell us you didn't know the dead man. This is your supposed, beloved husband."

"No, my husband was Ke—"

"Kenneth Lord," Benno finished for her.

He was looking at her as if he was sure she'd lost her mind. The truth hit her then—too much for her to take in. The air squeezed out of her lungs and her vision went fuzzy as her knees buckled under her.

BENNO FLEW TO CATCH Sydney before she could hit the ground. She was a light weight in his arms and he balanced her easily.

Worry for her competed with the shock of seeing his friend's body. What in hell was going on? he wondered wildly. Sydney had claimed Kenneth had gone off a cliff, but here he was, shot to death—as had been the man in her dream. Or had it really been a dream? he fleetingly wondered before realizing she'd seemed as shocked as he was.

He pulled her unconscious body tightly to his chest, his free hand stroking her face. "Sydney, tell me you're all right."

"Aren't you going to do anything?" Martha demanded of Brickman.

"That depends on what you mean. I'm going to hand the deceased over to the state police. They'll take the corpse to Portland to do the lab work."

"Kenneth has been shot dead. Any fool can see that."

Still cradling Sydney, Benno watched Martha carefully kneel next to the corpse as though she didn't want to get her clothes dirty. He thought she might touch her brother—but at the last second, she recoiled.

"I'm talking about procedure, Martha."

Two perfect tears rolled down her cheeks as she glared up at the policeman. "And I'm talking about justice."

Brickman stooped and slipped what could be interpreted as a steadying arm around her. Benno recognized the gesture as one more intimate and was surprised that Martha didn't move away, that she actually allowed the policeman to hold her tightly after pulling her to her feet.

"I'll take care of getting justice, too." Brickman sucked in his gut, stood taller, made his voice reassuring. "Be patient for a little while longer. The lab technicians are experts. They'll find the evidence we need to catch the murderer."

"I don't need any evidence to know who did this!"

Benno's attention came back to Sydney who stirred in his arms. Her eyes fluttered open. First they were filled with confusion, then horror.

She grabbed at his shirtfront with desperate fingers. "That isn't Kenneth!"

"But it is. Was," Benno corrected, studying her intently.

She shook her head wildly and struggled to get her balance. Then she pushed herself out of his arms. "That's not the same Kenneth Lord I married."

Benno heard the conviction in her words. If she hadn't married the Kenneth Lord that lay here dead, then who had she married?

"Finally, we get something called truth here." Pulling herself free from Brickman, Martha attacked. "I knew Kenneth would never have committed himself to some stranger without telling me. Now all we need is justice. What was your scheme, anyway? An elaborate plan to kill my brother and then plead a nervous breakdown? Why? Did you really think I'd let you have his money?''

"Benno?" Sydney choked. "There must be some kind of explanation."

Benno couldn't help his tight-lipped response. He wanted to believe her...but Kenneth had been his friend. He truly didn't know what to think.

"I'm afraid things look bad for you," Brickman said, earning a grateful look from Martha. "You told us your husband went over the cliff. You should have stuck to your story and buried the body."

"My husband *did* go over the cliff! I've never seen this man before in my life—not until the dream."

Her forehead wrinkled and her head tilted to one side as she seemed to be searching deeply within herself.

Benno looked from her to Kenneth and noticed his right hand was curled into a fist. Curious, he picked up the dropped flashlight, stooped over the body, and, with difficulty, pried open his friend's fingers. He flashed the beam over the palm and from it, freed a small piece of metal that had stuck to Kenneth's skin.

"Don't touch that!" Brickman ordered too late.

The triangular-shaped piece of metal was already in Benno's hand. "Looks like a stud."

"Shouldn't have done that." Brickman produced a handkerchief. "Now your fingerprints are on it."

Benno dropped the object into the handkerchief, which Brickman stuffed into his pocket.

"Trying to cover for the lady here?" the policeman asked.

"I didn't do anything wrong," Sydney protested, her voice rising with each word.

Brickman grunted. "Let's get back to the house so I can make the necessary calls. In the meantime, we'll be investigating you more closely, Mrs. . . . uh, Miss Raferty. Don't even consider doing a disappearing act."

Benno saw how stricken Sydney was. Emotions rushed to the fore and he set a protective arm around her; she had a pull on him he couldn't deny. His head was whirling as they picked their way back over the grounds.

"Can't you just arrest her and lock her up in one of your jail cells?" Martha pleaded with Brickman. "I refuse to have a murderer under my roof."

"No one has proved Sydney is a murderer," Benno stated.

When Martha flashed him a look of pity, he frowned. Maybe it was he who was losing his mind. What if he was getting himself tangled up with a woman capable of committing murder?

SYDNEY FELT AS IF she were trapped in a nightmare. This couldn't be happening to her.

Her husband not her husband.

Dead but not dead.

Even Benno didn't seem to believe her this time.

She sat frozen on the sofa for hours, while police came and went and the bagged body of the real Kenneth Lord was taken away. The murder site was cordoned off until it could be properly searched and photographed in daylight by evidence technicians.

Sydney was questioned; copious notes were taken. Over and over, she reiterated everything that had happened from the first moment she'd met the man she now knew to be an impostor, to the moment when she'd stumbled over the corpse of the real Kenneth Lord. When she tried to explain the dream, she was looked at with a combination of pity and disbelief. Even though the authorities didn't immediately arrest her, she got the feeling they already had her tried and convicted.

Again, she was warned not to leave town. The police left just before midnight.

Martha flounced off to the police station with Officer Brickman, saying she would be back, but if she had to share her house with a murderess for even one night, she would be sure to lock her door and "protect" herself if necessary. Then Sydney was left with Benno. She waited for him to abandon her, too. And how could she blame him?

Instead, he stood in the shadows, leaning on a windowsill, staring out into the dark.

"You don't believe me anymore," she said quietly.

"You have to admit it would take a real stretch of the imagination to give your story credibility."

"It's much easier to believe I invented a marriage and a husband, then killed Kenneth Lord and called the police only to claim I never saw the dead man before." She could hardly keep her voice from shaking. "Right?"

He turned to her, his face deep in shadow. "That doesn't make sense, either."

"Not even if I thought I could make big money on some grand scheme Martha thinks I concocted?"

"Not even then."

"Maybe I have gone around the bend," Sydney said as much to herself as to him. "Maybe I'm crazy and had no motive. Maybe I can't tell fantasy from reality anymore.''

Even as she made the charges against herself, Sydney wasn't convinced. Before finding the body, she had gone over every detail of her romance with "Kenneth Lord." Everything had to have happened just as she'd said.

Her mind was filled with memories, not delusions.

Benno was silent for a moment before asking, "Do you have any enemies?"

"What?"

"Someone who would want to set you up?"

Blinking, startled by the thought, she tried to make out his expression, which she thought serious enough. "No. I don't think so. Set me up for what—murder?"

He shrugged. "If you really did marry someone claiming to be Kenneth Lord—"

"I did!" she said vehemently, not realizing until that moment how very certain she was.

Sounding more sure of her, he offered, "Then you may have been the victim of a con."

"Conned?" Her mind began spinning again. The Kenneth Lord she'd met and married had been an impostor. That was an irrefutable fact. So what else did that make her erstwhile husband but a con man? "For what purpose?"

"To provide a patsy to take the fall when the real Kenneth Lord was killed?"

"If you're correct . . ." Her hand went to her throat and she took a deep, shaky breath. "I can't for the life of me think of who would hate me so much."

"Or hate Kenneth." Benno seemed to be deep in thought. "Perhaps you were merely . . . available. You were burned out, feeling fragile, and our murderer recognized your susceptibility when he met you.''

With each word Benno uttered, Sydney's anger grew. Yes, she had been experiencing burnout as a result of the stresses of her job. And the dreams had disturbed her even more. Because she hadn't been prepared to acknowledge these psychic warnings, she had multiplied the pressure on herself.

''But why? Who would want to take such advantage of me?'' And another thought crystallized. ''He's still alive. The man who married me is alive. He must be, right? He had to have been part of some elaborate scheme. He might be the murderer.''

''A man pretending to be Kenneth falls off a cliff—and somehow manages to survive to kill the real Kenneth Lord.''

''Sounds crazy. How could he have engineered such a fall? How will I ever convince the authorities he somehow managed it?'' Her situation seemed hopeless. ''Without proof, they'll continue to think I'm crazy or a murderer—or both.''

From the depths of her soul, Sydney drew on the very essence of her true nature. Her innate resilience had been bruised and battered, but she hadn't lost it yet. Anger, hot and sharp, jolted her into a frame of mind that gave her an inner strength, a state of certainty, a sense of purpose that she hadn't felt in months.

Remembering the premonition that had turned into frightening reality—that of her husband calling her to join him in death—she calmly said, ''I'm going to find him if it's the last thing I ever do.''

Benno drew closer. ''How do you propose to accomplish that when you don't even know who *he* is?''

At least he wasn't questioning whether the man even existed. "I don't, but somehow I must find out."

"If these speculations are correct."

In tune with her instincts, Sydney felt they were on the right track. "So many questions to be answered." She stared at Benno who now loomed over her. "One way or another, I'm going to find out. I'm going to prove my innocence and sanity to all of you."

His expression was unreadable when he said, "Sounds as though you've lumped me in with the others."

"Aren't you?"

"It would be a first."

For all the time she'd spent with this man during the past few days, for as well as she'd grown to know him and as much as she'd come to care for him, Sydney couldn't believe she was just now realizing how far he was from fitting into the big picture around Stone Beach. She'd been too self-absorbed, too immersed in her own troubles to realize the ramifications of his being at odds not only with Martha, but with Mick Brickman and Parnell Anderson, as well.

But the real Kenneth Lord had been his friend.

"As cockeyed as your story sounds," Benno was saying, "I want to believe you."

"That's something, then."

Probably more than she should have hoped for, given the circumstances. Even she had thought she was losing her mind.

"But what I think doesn't count for much around here," he went on, confirming her suspicions. "My being on your side might hurt you in the long run."

For the life of her, Sydney couldn't figure out why and she felt as if she didn't have the right to ask. She sensed his reasons were very private, and that his hurt ran very deep. If Benno wanted her to know the source of his trouble with the town, no doubt he would tell her in due time.

She realized how permanent that sounded, as if they would be allies forever, when she, in fact, was eager to leave Stone Beach as soon as she cleared her name. The thought of being without Benno left her with a sense of loss she couldn't quite comprehend.

Edgy, she rose and paced the length of the living room. "If I could pick anyone in the world to be on my side," she assured him honestly, "that person would be you."

A hint of a smile softened Benno's granitelike features. "That's quite an endorsement."

"A sincere one."

"So where do we start?" When she stopped her pacing and raised her eyebrows in question, he said, "Kenneth was my friend, you know. An accident is one thing, murder quite another."

Suddenly she became aware of the grief that Benno was feeling—the grief that she had claimed as her own for the past several days. All that was changed now. She was freed of one cause for suffering, filled with another. Now she had a different reason to mourn.

Hers had become a loss of innocence.

"I wasn't even thinking of him," she admitted softly.

Discovering the identity of the dead man must have come as quite a shock to Benno, much more so than when she'd first told him about the accident. Bodies lost at sea were so much less tangible than ones riddled with bullets and covered with blood. She herself was still shaken, albeit for a variety of different reasons.

"Benno, I'm so sorry."

Their eyes met as they shared a quiet moment in which words weren't necessary.

Then he broke the silence. "So where do we start?" he asked again, his tone more positive this time.

"There's the justice of the peace who married us...." Her voice faltered. "My God, I'm married to a man whose name I don't even know."

"If the marriage is even considered legal, considering the circumstances. You think the J.P. will be able to tell you something?"

"I won't know until I ask him."

"Until *we* ask him. I'm going with you." He cut off any objection by adding, "You're not supposed to leave town, remember? We'll sneak you out in my car and get you back before anyone misses you."

Though Sydney could tell Benno still had some reservations, he was giving her the benefit of the doubt. She couldn't ask for more.

"All right, we'll do this together. I appreciate the offer. The excursion will have to wait until morning." She looked around. "But we don't have to. Maybe we can find some of the answers right here."

"You mean search the house. I don't have the faintest idea what we'd be looking for. Do you?"

She shrugged. "Anything out of the ordinary. At least it'll keep us busy. I am certainly in no mood to sleep." Realizing he'd left his business to come to her when she'd called, Sydney said, "Sorry, I'm not thinking. You should get back—"

"Poppy can take care of things," he interrupted. "I'll call and explain."

Happy that she wouldn't be abandoned, she said, "I'm really going to owe you one—Lord, I owe you now."

"No. Kenneth was my friend. And now you are." His expression was grim, intensely personal. "I want to get to the bottom of this just as much as you do."

Once again Sydney was struck by whatever it was Benno *wasn't* saying. "Why don't you go through Kenneth's study while I check Martha's room before she returns."

"You'd better be careful. If she even suspects you've gone through her things, there'll be hell to pay."

Sydney laughed. "I've been to hell and back in less than a week. I'm not afraid of Martha."

"Perhaps you should be...."

If Martha were the murderer? Sydney silently finished. The smile died on her lips.

"Benno, too much has happened to me, too much is at stake for me to sit by and idly watch what's left of my life be destroyed. I'm ready to take on anyone to learn the truth. Even a murderer."

With that, she headed for the stairs.

"So we're looking for anything out of the ordinary," Benno muttered. "Now if only we can figure out what that is."

He disappeared inside Kenneth's office as she reached the landing.

Sydney tried to keep her mind off Benno and on her purpose as she entered Martha's room and snapped on the light switch. He was helping her for Kenneth's sake, she told herself, and simply because he was a good man, a caring human being. She was his friend—

he'd told her as much—and she needed to be content with that. She might want more from Benno, but at this point she had too many doubts about her own judgment.

Furthermore, there could be no second-guessing the future until the present was settled.

With that in mind, she tried to look at the room she disliked so much with fresh eyes. But nothing had changed. Sydney saw Martha's stamp on every item.

So what did that tell her? That Martha Lord was greedy and liked to put on airs. These facts did not make her a murderer. Sydney did not know whether Martha was capable of concocting an elaborate scheme to get her brother out of the way for his money—or of hiring and coaching an impostor who would seduce a vulnerable stranger and set her up for a fall.

A chill shot through Sydney as the phrasing reminded her of her own close call with death the night before last; she quickly checked the balcony doors to make sure they were locked. Even though she couldn't be manipulated again, she didn't want any nasty surprises.

Once she was sure the room was secured, she started to search the mirrored dresser. She tried not to think about the man she'd known as Kenneth, a man she'd been convinced she loved, one who might have seduced her to her death on that balcony.

Would the police have found a suicide note along with her and the real Kenneth Lord's bodies?

She concentrated on her search. The glass-covered dresser top held nothing but the finest creams and lotions and perfumes. A quilted satin and velvet box cradled expensive costume jewelry and a few smaller pieces of real gold set with gems. The drawers overflowed with luxurious lingerie and designer accessories. Having occasionally shopped on Rodeo Drive herself, Sydney recognized the labels. Martha certainly had a taste for the extravagant.

Extravagant enough to want all her brother's money? she wondered again. While the woman had put up a good front earlier, playing the role of the grief-stricken sister, Sydney hadn't felt any genuine emotion coming from her. And she'd noticed Martha hadn't once touched her brother's body.

Making sure everything was again neatly in place, Sydney slid the last drawer closed.

She decided to check the desk next. The only understated expensive piece of furniture in the room, the desk was actually a spindly-legged writing table with a row of pigeonholes in the back and a single drawer in front. There was nothing understated about the jewel-encrusted gold clock sitting on its surface—its hands indicated the hour was 12:19—nor about the mother-of-pearl and gold pen, which lay across heavy cream-colored stationery emblazoned with Martha's name in gold letters.

Noting the faint indentations in the top sheet of paper made Sydney curious.

When she picked it up, the fancy pen rolled off the paper and onto the top of the desk. Carefully, she picked up the pen and set it back exactly as she'd found it.

Whatever Martha had last written had pressed through to the sheet of paper in her hand. Before she could figure out how to tell what that might have been, she heard the Porsche pull up in the driveway.

"Damn!"

Hoping Benno had heard, as well, she leaped for the light switch, threw the room into darkness and left before Martha could catch her playing detective. Folding and stuffing the piece of paper into a pocket, she hurried across the landing and was just coming down the stairs when Martha entered the house.

"What are you still doing here?" Martha demanded, though she wasn't looking at Sydney.

Benno stood at the liquor cabinet where he was casually pouring himself a drink. "Having a nightcap. Want something?"

"I want you to leave!" The expression she turned from him to Sydney was ice-cold. "And you—I expect you to be out of my house first thing tomorrow. I still don't understand why you weren't arrested."

"The police didn't find any evidence to implicate Sydney," Benno said. "And she doesn't have a clear-cut motive. How about you?"

For a moment, Martha was speechless. Then she sputtered, "K-Kenneth was my b-brother!"

"And we all know how much you loved him, don't we?"

Martha bristled. "Get out. Now!"

Benno looked questioningly at Sydney.

"I'll be all right," she said.

"*You'll* be?" Martha muttered, sounding genuinely worried. She rushed for the staircase. "I'm the one who has reason to be afraid. Just don't try anything, Sydney, or you'll be sorry."

"What does that mean?" Benno asked. "Do you have a gun?"

Martha almost tripped, then caught herself. She sped up the stairs without looking back in their direction.

"Do you think she does?" Sydney asked, suddenly wondering if it was a good idea to stay in the same house with Martha for even a single night. "I didn't have time to check everything."

"Neither did I. And now we can't do anything without raising her suspicions. Knowing Martha, she'd call the police and demand they arrest us for attempted theft."

"Given the circumstances, she might succeed."

"I guess we'll have to call it a night," Benno said. "I don't think you have any real reason to worry about Martha doing you harm—though I expect you to make sure you're safely locked in your own room when I leave."

Remembering the paper in her pocket, Sydney dug it out. "Don't leave yet." She looked around. "I need a pencil."

"On the coffee table."

She hurried to the table where she smoothed the paper out on the wooden surface. She used the graphite edge of the pencil to lightly color in the impressions.

"What are you doing?" Benno asked.

"Finding out what Martha wanted to tell someone," Sydney whispered. "Look," she said, as the indentations turned into a message that was faint but clear against the smudged graphite.

She tilted the paper to the light so they could read it:

Meet me at midnight.

M.

Chapter Seven

"If only we could figure out which night Martha sent the note," Benno said as he turned onto Three Capes Loop and headed for the beachtown of Oceanside the next morning.

They hadn't given up speculating about the damn thing. Sydney swore Martha had been elsewhere the previous two midnights. Had she returned from the rendezvous while they'd been conducting their search? Or had the meeting been set up for the night before that—when Kenneth was murdered? Rather after Sydney had had the dream? The police had not yet confirmed the time of Kenneth's death. Sydney claimed Martha had come home around one that night. She was certain of the time because she'd checked the clock when he'd returned her call from the coffeehouse.

"If only we knew to whom Martha sent the message." Sydney sighed. "She would avoid identifying the person. The way she's been hanging onto Officer Brickman, wouldn't it be ironic if the two of them were having secret trysts and she's been with the 'law' instead of breaking it."

"Martha with Brickman?" Benno couldn't fathom that one, but he never had been able to figure out why Poppy had married the man, either. Mick Brickman must hold some mysterious power over women. "And what about our impostor—maybe she was meeting him."

"I don't know. I only hope we're about to find out."

Almost forty miles south of Stone Beach, they passed Cape Meares, the first of three state parks with world-class seascape views. Not that Benno could enjoy them. He was worrying that someone might have seen them leave town. He hoped not. He wanted to have some answers and Sydney back to the house before anyone missed her. Her bags were packed and she had already reserved a room at a local motel.

"Did you by any chance use up the milk?" Sydney asked, the change of topic startling him.

"Milk?"

"You know, the stuff I warmed up and drank the first evening I spent in the house."

"No. I'm not a milk drinker myself."

"Someone did. Or threw away half a carton. It was gone when I went to fix myself another glass the following night."

Recognizing her speculative tone, Benno flashed her a glance. "What are you getting at?"

"I've been thinking about your assumption that I'd taken sedatives or sleeping pills. I hadn't. No one could have drugged the milk in the glass because it was never out of sight, but what if someone drugged the carton, then got rid of the evidence?"

"Someone who knew about your nighttime habit?"

"Kenneth—the impostor—did."

Benno hadn't considered the possibility that someone else had drugged her. Why should he have? But now he had to admit the idea had some merit if this theory about her having been set up was correct.

"That would account for your confusion and shakiness."

"And for that overwhelming feeling of unreality."

Benno hoped they were going to get some answers—and soon—as they entered the breezy hamlet of Oceanside.

"We took pictures here after..." Sydney's voice trailed off.

She was staring out at the ocean toward Three Arch Rocks National Wildlife Refuge, home to a large sea lion community.

"If only I had those photographs," she murmured. "How did he get hold of them?"

Figuring she meant the impostor, Benno didn't respond. He had his own speculations about the switch of the photographs. Donald Norridge, the clerk at the photo shop, was Parnell Anderson's second cousin. If Parnell were involved...

Benno was withholding the information from Sydney. He didn't feel comfortable dredging up the past, not unless he found some reason to believe Kenneth was murdered for it. Meanwhile, he had to keep an open mind. He wasn't absolutely certain about Sydney's credibility; as much as he wanted to believe her, he still had his doubts.

"Turn up ahead," she told him.

She guided him to a modest house set back from town on a gravel road in the midst of a stand of Sitka spruce and western red cedar. The undergrowth was a tangle of salal and Pacific wax myrtle with clumps of wildflowers where the sun streamed in. The place looked comfortable, if well-weathered and in need of repair as were many of the wooden structures along the coast.

The first thing Sydney said when she left the car was, "The sign is gone. There was a sign over the mailbox—Thomas Suchet, Justice of the Peace."

Benno heard the panic in her voice, saw it in her eyes as she turned her stricken gaze to him. Despite the warnings he'd given himself to be cautious, he took her hand and gave it a reassuring squeeze. He sensed her apprehension subside a bit, but still she clasped his hand as if it were a lifeline when they stopped in front of the door. A small tag on the mailbox identified the occupant as T. Suchet. That was encouraging, Benno thought as he knocked.

When no immediate response to the knock came, he could feel the anxiety well up in Sydney once more.

"Oh, God . . . he's probably not even here."

Positive he heard movement inside, Benno knocked again, louder this time. "Anyone home?" he called.

"Yeah, yeah, coming."

The thin, stooped man who opened the door was elderly and grizzled. Suspenders over a white V-neck T-shirt held up a pair of trousers that had seen better days. He took in his visitors and Benno caught the flicker of recognition in his watery hazel eyes before he slipped on a pair of wire-rimmed glasses.

"What can I do for you folks?" he asked pleasantly.

"You can—"

"Let us in," Benno cut in smoothly. "So we can talk in private."

"I don't think so."

Suchet tried to slam the door in their faces, but Benno held out a hand that stopped him.

"Talk to us. Please, this is important."

A moment's indecision. The man shifted his gaze back to Sydney, then grunted. He turned his back on them and shuffled to an armchair in the narrow living room.

"You do remember me, don't you, Mr. Suchet?" Sydney asked as he sat.

"I remember. You two aren't going to give me grief, are you?" He ran a hand through his mussed hair. "I don't need the law on my back. I live a nice, quiet life here."

"No police," Benno bargained, "If you cooperate."

"How do you know me, Mr. Suchet?" Sydney asked.

"Huh?"

"I want you to explain how we met."

"You know perfectly well—"

"But *I* don't," Benno said, giving Sydney credit for having her wits about her. Rather than prompting the man with what she wanted everyone to believe, she was letting Suchet come up with the explanation.

The elderly man was silent for a moment, then seemed to make up his mind. "I met the young lady last week when I performed her marriage ceremony," Suchet stated.

So that was the truth, Benno thought with relief. "To whom?"

"Some guy named Kenneth Lord."

Sydney's drawn breath was audible. She went almost limp with relief. Benno gave her an encouraging look before turning back to Suchet.

"Who was the man?" Benno asked.

"I just told you."

"I mean his real name. The man you met wasn't Kenneth Lord."

Suchet seemed neither surprised nor unnerved by the information. "Maybe not, but he didn't give me no other name."

He sounded as if he was telling the truth.

"So I *am* married to a man whose name I don't even know," Sydney said faintly.

Benno narrowed his gaze menacingly and loomed over the elderly man. "Is she?"

Uncertainty flickered in his eyes behind the thick lenses. Suchet licked his lips. "Uh, not exactly."

"What?"

"I'm not a justice of the peace anymore. It's been some years actually." His frightened gaze met Benno's. "I, uh, am no longer empowered to marry anyone. You're not going to call the police on me, are you?"

Benno realized the old guy was afraid and seemed harmless. He figured they'd get the truth out of him with a little prompting.

"Depends," he said.

"Look, I didn't mean no harm. I thought of it like an acting job."

"So you were hired to perform the ceremony. Why you?"

"Kenneth Lord or whatever his name is heard about me from someone in town. He came to me a few days before the wedding and asked me if I'd like to make a couple hundred bucks. I'm not a rich man. I didn't see the harm," he reiterated, worrying the arm of the chair with trembling fingers.

"You didn't see any harm in letting me think I was married?" Sydney indignantly demanded. "Didn't you realize that that man might have meant to do me harm?"

Shaking now, Suchet couldn't meet her eyes. "I kind of felt sorry for you. I did. But I needed the money. And I thought it was some kind of joke."

Benno wasn't convinced of that, no matter how contrite the elderly man seemed now. Thomas Suchet had known performing the fake marriage was wrong, but he'd been tempted by the money. A couple of hundred bucks to ruin another person's life—the idea boggled Benno's mind.

Pulling a business card from his wallet, he held it out. "Here's my number. If you remember anything else—or if you see the man who hired you around town—call me." He couldn't help adding, "You need money, I've got it. No joke."

Suchet took the card but didn't look up. Shame resonating in his voice, he said, "I don't want your money. If I remember anything, I'll call."

Every last doubt about Sydney's innocence burned away, Benno grasped her elbow and propelled her through the open door. He didn't speak as he led her to the car.

His mind was spinning.

Sydney set up. Kenneth dead. What was the motive?

Sydney suspected Martha was after her brother's money, but then she didn't now all the facts. She didn't know about Parnell Anderson and his sick hatred.

But *he* knew. Parnell could have been waiting all those years for an opportunity to exact the revenge he'd sworn to get.

And now Kenneth was dead.

And, if his suspicions were correct, Sydney wasn't the only one in trouble.

SYDNEY'S SENSE OF RELIEF was so overwhelming she felt as if her bones would melt as she lay her head back against the bucket seat. Suddenly the beauty of the day with its blue sky, white clouds and brilliant yellow sun struck her. She took in a deep breath of fresh air lightly scented by the nearby ocean.

"Do you think we should stop in town and call the police, tell them about Suchet?" she asked as they backtracked the gravel road.

"Let's wait until we see what else we find. You're not even supposed to have left town, remember?"

"True. And maybe we won't have to involve him," she said. "Although I don't know why I should feel sorry for the man."

"I don't, either. If he hadn't played along—"

"My fake Kenneth would have found someone else to do the job," Sydney stated.

They were both lost in thought until Benno turned the car back onto the road to town.

"By the way, who witnessed the wedding?" he asked. "Maybe we can get more information from them."

"I don't think either witness would know more than Suchet since he provided them. One was an elderly friend of his named Agnes who played the piano—she was hard of hearing. The other was a ditsy young woman named Tippy who cleans house for him."

"Hmm, not promising leads. So much for that idea."

For a while Sydney sat quietly thinking. She resented that she was visited by dreams and visions and premonitions when she didn't want to be but couldn't even use her "gifts" to prove her own innocence.

"I know he's alive," she said, breaking the silence. "There must be some way we can find him."

Benno sounded a little odd when he suggested, "We could check out the place you two were staying before you got married."

"We weren't exactly staying together."

Sydney grew hot with embarrassment. She felt bad enough that Benno knew a con man had tricked her into marrying him, but having to admit how successful he'd been in seducing her was something she didn't want to think about, no less talk about. At least not with Benno.

No matter how much she wanted to deny it—no matter how many times she reminded herself she'd been in love with "Kenneth"—her feelings for Benno were growing, and there was nothing she could do to stop that from happening. It was as if knowing she really hadn't been married to his friend—hadn't been married to anyone—had set her emotions free.

"I mean, the whole thing happened so quickly," she went on, giving him a sideways glance. "The romance was whirlwind, the marriage impulsive. He didn't spend much time at his hotel in Lincoln City, but he, um, never actually registered at The Cascades where I was staying."

She hoped her evasive answer would satisfy him.

He took a moment to digest her statement before asking, "So there's no other place we could go to check out someone who might be able to give us a lead?''

Sydney thought hard. "We had casual contacts, but no one who seemed to really know Ken . . . uh, him.''

"So much for that idea.''

As they drove back through town, Sydney suddenly remembered something they could check.

"The car. I forgot all about his car. The day we got married, we used mine. He said he'd been having trouble starting his and didn't want to chance spoiling our wedding day with a breakdown. So we left it in the parking lot at my hotel with the intention of picking it up the next day. Of course taking care of a vehicle was the last thing on my mind after I thought I'd lost a husband.''

"Chances are it'll have disappeared as conveniently as its owner. Or it might have been impounded by now.''

"What have we got to lose but a little time?'' Sydney asked, her excitement growing. "Maybe he never planned to go back for the car. Maybe it's still there and we can find out who he is through the registration.''

"It's worth a shot,'' Benno agreed, though he sounded far from convinced.

This time when they passed Three Arch Rocks, Sydney averted her gaze. Throughout the past days, she'd experienced a gamut of emotions—grief, fear, anger. Now sadness colored her view. She'd been full of positive daydreams of the future when she'd posed for a photo in front of the wildlife refuge. Every woman should be able to remember her wedding day as the happiest of her life. Now that hers had been exposed as nothing but a sham she felt cheated. A lump stuck in her throat.

As if he sensed her inner turmoil, Benno reached over and covered her hand with his. Sydney sent him a swift glance. He didn't take his eyes from the road, but she would have sworn his granitelike features softened a bit. Unsettled by an attraction she wasn't yet and might never be ready to act on, she nevertheless gave him directions to The Cascades, a resort near Lincoln City, without letting on. He considered her a friend, she reminded herself, and she couldn't ask for a better one.

Yet Benno didn't remove his hand from hers until they entered the resort's grounds.

And Sydney steeled herself for what was to come.

The Cascades was an environmentalist's dream come true, one of several such resorts developed and financed by Reynard Stirling, wealthy industrialist and the Pacific Northwest's most ardent and outspoken environmentalist. The magnificent setting—seven hundred and fifty acres between endless ocean and primeval forest—was inspiring and romantic.

Here, Sydney had foolishly fallen in love.

"Keep to the right," she said, unprepared for the intensity of the memories the place inspired.

Sydney hadn't thought returning to The Cascades would be such a painful experience, not after being disillusioned so thoroughly. She only hoped time would have the power to heal her wounds.

"How far do I go?" Benno asked.

"Um." For a moment she was confused, all the guest buildings looking alike because of the covered walkways connecting them. Then she spotted the giant Sitka with the split trunk that had been part of her view. "Two buildings ahead. Take the driveway to the rear."

"It's the silver Oldsmobile." She pointed to the loner at the back of the lot as a thought struck her. "That isn't the real Kenneth Lord's car, is it?"

"Nope. Kenneth drove a Saab."

Benno pulled the Thunderbird alongside the more conservative automobile. When they checked its doors, they found all were locked.

Chagrined, Sydney said, "I hadn't thought about how we were going to get inside."

"We may have to break in."

"You know how to do that?"

"Let me count the ways."

Wondering where he'd learned such tricks, Sydney frowned as Benno circled the car and ran his hand under the wheel wells and bumpers. She really didn't know anything about the man's background, but she didn't feel as if she was in a position to question it now.

"I think we should go to the lobby, to Guest Services. I could make up some story—I'm certain guests occasionally lock themselves out of their cars."

"That won't be necessary." At the rear passenger wheel, Benno straightened. He held a set of keys in his hand. "Key magnets—a car thief's delight."

Sydney couldn't help wondering if Benno had ever stolen a car himself. She shoved the unpleasant thought away. She'd had enough experience with dishonesty to last her a lifetime.

"Why don't we start by looking for the registration," she suggested.

Obliging her, Benno unlocked the passenger door and opened the glove compartment. "The only document in here is the owner's manual." He pulled it out and flipped through the pages, then held the booklet by one cover and shook. "Nope, no registration, no insurance card."

"You're not surprised."

"Can't say that I am."

"So let's see what else we can find."

Benno unlocked the driver's door for her. Sydney started searching every niche of that side and worked her way to the back seat.

Just as thoroughly, Benno probed the passenger side. "Not a thing," he said when he'd finished his search.

"Nothing," she agreed. "Maybe we'll get lucky in the trunk."

He leaned across the passenger seat and hit a button hidden in the glove compartment. The trunk lid popped up and Sydney circled to the rear of the car. The interior was loaded.

"This'll keep us busy for a while," Benno said, digging into the mess.

In order to get to the bottom of the trunk, they had to empty it. Within minutes, the contents were spread along the ground behind the car. They knelt and carefully inspected each item. They sorted through pillows and a blanket, a gym bag containing smelly running shoes and exercise clothes, a toolbox, a plastic bag filled with hangers, fast-food wrappers and assorted small items equally valueless.

No name tags, no IDs of any kind.

"Nothing," Sydney said in disgust. "What now?"

"Load her back up before someone sees us, I guess." Benno rose. With fists balled on his hips, he stared into the trunk as if he could conjure up the information they sought. "Hang on a second."

He did a more thorough inspection of the trunk's empty interior—the wells behind the brake lights, a small storage compartment empty save for jumper cables, the open area under the back seat. Finally, he lifted the rug that covered the recessed spare tire and ran his hands around the well.

Balancing the pillows and blanket on the fender, Sydney heard a crinkling noise as Benno pulled out a wad of brown paper.

Shaking his head, he straightened the crumpled bag. "The guy's a real pig. We can use this for his garbage."

Sydney dumped the bedding into the empty trunk as he bent over and reached for some of the fast-food wrappers. A small rectangular piece of blue paper floated from the mouth of the bag. Benno's hand flashed out and caught the slip before it hit the ground.

About to shove it back into the bag, he turned the piece of paper over. "A register tape."

Sydney moved close. Although her side was pressed against his, she still couldn't make out the figures. "The ink's so light you can hardly read anything."

"This is the important part," he said, tapping the line at the top. "*S-E*. A couple of blanks. *I-D-E*. Then, a second word. *L*. Blank. *Q*. More blanks. Liquor? Something Liquor," he said with more certainty.

Sydney tried putting the letters together. "Se—ide Liquor."

"Seaside Liquor! What do you think?"

Tempted to hug Benno, she restrained herself. "That must be it." Instead, she stepped back to safety.

Too late. His voice lowered to a throb when he said, "We make some team."

Sydney stared into light brown eyes that sizzled with the same excitement she was feeling. She wondered which had provoked the greater reaction—the lead they'd found or the "some team" part? Her pulse skittered through her as she speculated. Friends, she reminded herself. They were friends.

Trouble was she was feeling more than friendly.

Trouble was she had felt that way about the fake Kenneth Lord only a week ago.

Tearing her eyes from Benno's, feeling the pulse beating strongly in her throat, she concentrated on the register tape in his hand. "Seaside is so close to Stone Beach that our mystery man could easily have been staying there while keeping an eye on me." Benno's eyes were still on her, making Sydney's heart pound. "Can you read the date?"

She needed a distraction. She would be foolish to get too close to any man now. No more whirlwind courtships.

"July something."

"I met him in July," she said, sobering. "We've got to go to Seaside to find him."

"If he's even there now. And Seaside isn't nearly as small as Stone Beach, you know, and at this time of year it's loaded with tourists. We can check the liquor store, but—"

"We can check the liquor store," she repeated firmly. "That's a start."

Sydney told herself to remember what was important—her freedom and future well-being. She didn't need a distraction all wrapped up in a virile male package complete with beard stubble and long hair and a diamond in his ear. She didn't need a man who made her feel things she didn't want to feel right now, who filled her with confusion every time they got too close.

And yet she feared she did need Benno.

Focusing on his chin scar, she said, "And in the meantime, we can get the authorities to track down the registration of this car."

"It's probably stolen."

Frowning, she met his gaze. "Do you have an obsession with stolen vehicles or something?"

"Not anymore," he said, making her wonder whether or not he was teasing. "I'm just being practical. I don't think a felon would want a car traced to him—and I don't think we want the authorities in on this before necessary. You weren't supposed to leave town, remember? If we don't think this through, we may do something rash. I'll write down the license plate and serial numbers. Got a pen?"

"I think so."

Grateful for the distraction, Sydney fetched her shoulder bag from the Thunderbird. She dug through the interior. No pen. As she was about to say so, her fingers brushed the zippered compartment.

"My God, I forgot," she said, excitement rising once more. She retrieved the arcade token and held it out to him. "Look. Seagull on one side, boardwalk on the other. Where would you say this came from?"

"Seaside has a boardwalk." Benno took the token. "Where did you get this?"

"I found it on Kenneth's Lord's property the day after you saved me from falling off the deck. I went looking for the ring and found the token instead.

There were cigarette butts all around the area—the kind our impostor smokes.''

Benno turned the arcade coin in his fingers. ''Maybe we're about to find him, after all.''

Part of Sydney was looking forward to facing the man who'd so cruelly used her, part of her dreading the reunion. ''He was in my room that night, you know. My drugged milk theory explains a lot—why he was there one minute, gone the next.''

''Your reaction times would have been slowed if you had been drugged,'' Benno continued.

''He could have done anything while I was out, could have slipped a duplicate wedding ring on my nightstand to confuse me.'' She shuddered. ''He could have led me to my death…if you hadn't been around. You always seem to be around when I need you, Benno.''

''You aren't going gooey on me again, are you?''

She'd almost forgotten that ''gooey'' made him uncomfortable. ''How about if I save gooey for after we find the guy and turn him over to the cops,'' she said with a grin, the tension she'd been feeling moments earlier dissipating. ''But first we have to write down those numbers.'' She started to check her bag once more.

''I think there's a ballpoint in the glove compartment,'' Benno told her as he slammed shut the lid of the trunk.

''I'll get it.''

Sydney tried to open the glove compartment but it wouldn't budge. Benno must have replaced the owner's manual the wrong way. The thing was jammed shut.

''Great. Now it won't open. Give me the keys.''

When he handed them to her, she inserted the correct one in the lock for extra leverage. After sliding sideways in the passenger seat, she jiggled, tapped, then slammed the heel of her hand against the small door.

"Want me to try?" he asked.

"No," she said, gritting her teeth in determination. "Just give me a sec—"

The door unjammed as she gave a mighty tug—and in the process tore the entire compartment free of restraints. It flipped upside down, its meager contents spewing across the passenger floor.

"Great," she muttered again.

At least she'd found the ballpoint. Bending over to pick it up, she froze when another object that had rolled under the dash caught her eye.

She retrieved the mechanical pencil, not at all the cheap sort of writing instrument a person would normally put in a glove compartment.

"Is something wrong?" Benno asked, leaning over the open door to see.

Sydney shook her head. "The tape register, the token and now this. You know the old saying—three's a charm. Guess who this belongs to?"

She held out the object in question, its mother-of-pearl and gold casing glinting in the sunlight.

Chapter Eight

Benno took the expensive mechanical pencil from her. "A woman," he guessed.

"Give the man a gold star."

"Martha?"

Sydney nodded. "That's one half of a set. She used the other half to write the 'Meet me at midnight' note. I found the ballpoint pen with her stationery. Needless to say, its uniqueness caught my attention. Now we know there's a connection between her and our man."

"Not necessarily," Benno argued. "If the fake Kenneth was wandering around the house, he could have picked this up and carried it off."

"And Martha could have been in this car with her hired cohort." When Benno didn't respond, she asked, "Do you know something I don't? Or do you just refuse to believe Martha is guilty for some reason."

"Kenneth was her brother."

"Do you really believe she loved him?"

"Sometimes love and hate are emotions that easily get confused." Benno quickly busied himself jotting down the license plate number on the reverse side of the register tape. "I suspect Martha felt both for Kenneth."

Then he walked to the front of the car and looked through the windshield to find the vehicle identification number. He added that information to the tape, which he then stuck into his shirt pocket. He handed her the pencil and token.

"Let's lock up and get going."

Sydney had let him do the talking because she was getting that feeling again, the one that told her whatever Benno wasn't saying was more important than what he was. But if she questioned him too thoroughly, he would think she didn't trust him. She didn't want that kind of tension between them, not after all he'd done for her.

He secured the Olds. She slipped the pencil and token into the zippered compartment of her shoulder bag and climbed into the Thunderbird.

The drive to Seaside took the better part of an hour, enough time to do a lot of thinking about Martha's probable involvement and motive...about her own gullibility...about Benno's secretiveness.

Her tension was certainly building. Questions hung between them that she needed answered. How to ask them without destroying their growing bond?

She hadn't even come close to figuring it out by the time they arrived in overcrowded Seaside. At noon, the streets were packed with tourists and conventioneers shopping and eating and taking advantage of the sun. The parking lots were filled, eager beach-goers waiting for a spot so they could join the fun off the two-mile-long concrete promenade. After ten minutes of cruising and waiting, Benno finally found a spot.

"This place is a zoo," Sydney said, stretching as she climbed out of the car.

"A pretty spiffy zoo," Benno told her. "Seaside used to have a reputation of being a hurdy-gurdy hustler town, but it's really been cleaned up over the last few years. Now it's a respected resort town. I hardly recognized the place when I moved back from California."

California. Sydney stored away that bit of information and decided to go for more. "Why did you decide to come back?"

"I guess I wanted to prove something," Benno admitted before slickly changing subjects. "Let's find a telephone booth." Grabbing her elbow, he steered her through a crowd of teenagers. "You can find the address of the liquor store in the directory, while I call Stone Beach Police and give them the information about the car."

"Wait. You were the one who said no authorities."

"I'm going to do this without involving you."

The only reason Sydney cared whether or not the authorities knew they were investigating together was because she didn't want Benno to get in trouble, but she figured saying so wouldn't change his mind. They found a telephone outside a nearby drugstore. She thumbed through the phone book while he placed the call to the police.

"Yeah, Brickman, it's Benno DeMartino." He paused, then said, "I've been doing some investigating on my own." He listened for a moment. "Look, I checked out a car parked at The Cascades. Sydney told me the man pretending to be Kenneth Lord left it there. Put a tracer on it, would you?"

Sydney found the listing for Seaside Liquors and took note of the address while Benno described the car and read off the license plate and vehicle identification numbers.

"Don't worry, Brickman," Benno said dryly, "Sydney's not trying to do a disappearing act." He gave her an exasperated expression. "How would I know? Probably took a walk on the beach or something." His expression grew furious. "Don't send out the troops, for God's sake." Another silence was followed by, "All right, all right, she's with me. Promise not to put out an APB." A short pause and he said, "Seaside, but I'll have her home before dark." He slammed the receiver into its cradle.

Sydney immediately got on his case. "Why, Benno? Now you've identified yourself as an accessory."

"To what? This isn't exactly a prison break we're involved in. I figure it would make the most sense to be up-front considering he'd already guessed I had something to do with your disappearance—Martha already told him you were gone. Besides, it won't matter since I'm going to bring you back soon."

"Only if we come to a dead end," she stated firmly. "I'm not going to stop if there's a chance I can find the man who's trying to destroy my life."

Benno nodded.

Finding Seaside Liquors was easy enough. Unfortunately, neither the clerk nor the store owner could place the man Sydney described.

"Are you sure?" Sydney asked, trying not to get discouraged. "He had the kind of looks and manner that could charm the most resistant feminine heart."

The owner rolled his eyes as if he was exasperated. "Lady, every season we get dozens of smooth-talking

Romeos coming through this town looking for excitement. And you wanna know if I remember someone who bought a bottle of booze a month ago?'' He shook his head and walked toward the back of the store, muttering, ''Gimme a break.''

''Sorry,'' the clerk added, shrugging his thin shoulders.

Sydney dug out the arcade token and showed it to him. ''Does this look familiar?'' she asked.

He shook his head. ''There's plenty of game arcades in this town. That could be from any one of them. I wouldn't know. I hate pinball machines and video games myself.''

''Thanks anyway.''

The clerk dismissed them by focusing his attention on another customer. Discouraged that their first lead hadn't panned out, they quickly left the store.

Back on the street, Sydney said, ''Maybe we should get a map of the town, pinpoint the arcades or other places that might use tokens. What do you think?''

''That I want to get something to eat first.''

Her own stomach could use some reinforcement. ''You're right. This could be a long afternoon. We might not be home before dark, after all.''

They agreed on a dive farther along the street that boasted: Fifty Variations on the All-American Hot Dog.

Benno ordered three kinds of dogs, a large order of fries, a shake and a piece of apple pie, making Sydney wonder how he managed to stay in such good shape. No doubt if she asked, he would turn her question into a joke . . . or rather than talk about himself, he'd channel the discussion elsewhere.

The small place was crowded, but a man was just leaving a spot in the corner. They claimed the table and waited for their food. Having come up with a plan to get Benno to reveal more about himself, Sydney opened her shoulder bag and pulled out her tarot deck.

His eyebrows shot up as she slid the cards from their pouch. "You're going to mess with those things now?"

"Yep."

He appeared skeptical. "Don't tell me a reading is going to help us find out felon."

"Nope. I'm going to do *your* reading. You said you wanted me to," she quickly added when she realized he was about to object. "Don't worry, this won't take long." She pulled four cards from the deck. "I can read while we eat." And maybe she'd be clever enough to coax out some of those answers she'd been looking for. Without waiting for him to agree, she explained, "First I want you to choose a card to represent you."

Of the various methods of choosing the significator, she'd decided to use one in which the different categories of court cards—king, queen, knight and page—delineated sex and age. Having removed the four knights from the deck, she held them out to Benno faceup.

"Which of these are you most drawn to?" she asked.

He gave her a look that clearly conveyed he was only doing this to indulge her. Then he picked the Knight of Swords and set it on the table.

A thrill shot through Sydney as she remembered the reading she'd done for herself shortly before they'd met. She'd turned over the Knight of Swords and had assumed the card represented her "late husband." Of course, Benno hadn't had the entire deck to pick from, she told herself. He'd had a one-in-four chance of choosing that very card.

Still, he had chosen it.

Reinstating the remaining three knights, she shuffled the deck and set it in front of him. "Now you. While you shuffle, think of a question you'd like answered or a problem to which you'd like to work out a solution."

Benno made an expert job of it, leaving her with no doubts that this wasn't the first time he'd handled cards.

"What kind of cards do you play?" she asked. Even finding out about his recreational habits would be a start. "Poker? Blackjack?"

"'Go Fish.'"

But only if he was serious, of course. He answered as if she should have known better than ask, but she couldn't help prodding him further.

"If you want, you can tell me the question or problem—"

"I'd rather hear what *you* have to say." His gaze was intense. "Isn't that what this is about—showing off your stuff?"

"Not exactly." Sydney realized her plan might not be as easy to implement as she'd hoped. "Cut the deck in three using your left hand." When he hesitated, she explained, "It's nearest your heart."

"Okay." With his left hand, Benno deftly split the deck into three piles.

"Now put them together in any order you prefer."

"So what is the object of this exercise?" he asked as he complied.

"To appease your curiosity... and mine."

As she took the deck from him, his expression was enigmatic, making Sydney think he'd guessed what she was up to. She began laying out the Celtic Cross, keeping the cards to one side of the table so there would be room for the food. Even before organizing her thoughts, before looking at the whole picture, the spread made her uneasy. In addition to the significator, three additional cards held swords.

Worse, she'd turned up The Tower, which could be one of the most unfavorable cards in the deck.

"That bad?" Benno asked, studying her.

Realizing she was frowning, Sydney told herself to lighten up. "Give me time to absorb everything," she hedged.

"You absorb. I'll eat."

One of the employees delivered their order on a tray. She returned her attention to the cards while Benno took their plates and drinks from the kid and set them on the table.

"So start interpreting," he prompted as he picked up a hot dog in one hand, a couple of fries in the other.

Determined to get the best from her reading as always, Sydney decided to soften what she was feeling. Again, the cards had put her in a negative frame of mind. She started with Benno's present situation covered by the Two of Swords.

"You're experiencing a great deal of frustration at this time. Something is stopping you from going forward and resolving whatever it is that's been troubling you."

"I suppose this has to do with finding our mystery man," he speculated.

"You tell me—is that the problem you chose?"

Rather than answering, he merely said, "Go on."

No, she hadn't thought so. She sensed the problem was a lot closer to home for him. Next came the Two of Cups. "A new relationship is influencing the situation—"

"Relationship or romance?" he was quick to interject.

"Could be either." She wasn't eager to pursue that line of thought since she already had the distinct impression that she was the other half of the relationship. "You're not happy in your present situation, but change is coming...."

For the better or worse? Sydney wondered, hoping that her reading wasn't adding to whatever worries Benno already had. Again, she gave probing him more directly another shot.

"If you did tell me what you wanted to resolve, I could make this reading more accurate."

He grinned as he picked up his second hot dog. "I'm sure you could."

"You're making fun of me."

"I'm not. I'm merely enjoying my Wisconsin cheesedog," he claimed. "Cheddar, Muenster and Colby."

She picked up her own hot dog and tore into it with a vengeance.

When she continued to concentrate on her food and ignore the cards, he said, "I thought you could eat and read at the same time."

"Not when you won't take me seriously."

Normally she wouldn't be so sensitive, but normally she wouldn't have her own hidden agenda in doing a reading. Furthermore, she wasn't averse to stopping before she had to go on to the next card, which she viewed with a sense of foreboding.

"I promise to take you seriously." When Sydney didn't immediately respond, Benno urged, "Please, go on."

Compelled to do as he asked, she forgot about her food and reluctantly turned back to the spread.

"This next position deals with the distant past."

The Tower Card. Touching it briefly, she jerked her hand away when a sudden chill swept up her arm. Her head grew light, her palms clammy. She flashed Benno a quick look and noted that his gaze was riveted to the illustration, a tower being struck by lightning.

"The Tower represents some upheaval in your past," she said.

But Sydney sensed more than some minor disturbance. And she rejected the interpretation that there would be a possible startling revelation in his future. She envisioned calamity and a terrible personal crisis. A sense of loss so great the feeling engulfed her and made her throat close. She wasn't sure if the ominous vibrations were coming from the card or directly from the man himself.

"A terrible tragedy," she whispered, even as she tried to reason with herself to let it go.

She'd struck a nerve. Raw emotion flickered in the amber depths of Benno's eyes before he successfully shuttered himself from her.

"Great hot dogs, aren't they?" He picked up his third. "Better finish. They're getting cold."

Obviously he'd had enough.

Sydney attacked her food in silence though she couldn't stop herself from finishing the reading silently. Whatever had happened so long ago was still affecting Benno, still keeping him in a constant state of battle, at least within himself. She reckoned that was the reason he didn't let anyone get too close. She saw the potential for defeat, humiliation, possible inability to change.

Yet his most positive card was that of self. She'd dealt him Strength, revealing a quiet confidence rather than dominance, calm perseverance and determination, the ability to accept what life held for him. As always, rather than being gospel, the cards were merely a road map, subject to personal interpretation, and she could find both positive and negative in them—though there had been that one moment when she'd sensed some frightful event in his past.

"Does this fortune-telling stuff always get to you like this?" he asked, again in complete control.

Quickly swallowing, she set down the last of her hot dog. "My readings are rarely this involving, or I wouldn't have tried to do yours here in public. Occasionally I sense more than what the actual cards tell me." She hesitated only a second before pushing him further. "I was correct about something terrible having happened in the past, wasn't I?"

"Yeah, well it doesn't really matter," he said, digging into his apple pie.

But it did matter, she realized. He couldn't hide from her now—not at this moment. The tough dark knight's vulnerability had shown through barely long enough for her to recognize it, but recognize it she had.

The knowledge was hers and with it came some understanding of who Benno was. Not the day-to-day details, perhaps, but a greater picture of the man beneath the tough exterior. Now if only he would talk to her, tell her about his past so she could really understand in concrete terms and try to help him as he'd helped her.

Unable to stop herself, she reached for his hand. "Having someone to talk to can be a big relief sometimes."

He shrugged but there was no nonchalance in the gesture. "So talk."

"I have been for days now. I can listen, too."

She could tell he was torn between wanting to reveal more and wanting to mask himself again.

"My past isn't anything to brag about. I was an unhappy kid who made others unhappy in return."

"Sounds like a kid thing to do. But you're a man now, and from what I know of you, you're kind, gentle, loyal—"

"Sounds as if you're talking about a dog."

A smile hovered around his mouth, prompting hers in return. "I'm talking about a man whom I like and respect very much," Sydney stated simply.

"You really don't know me."

"Not as much as I would like to, no, but you could fix that. Start with something easy—say, like why you decided to open Benno's Place."

He withdrew his hand from hers and she realized that her question was more loaded than she'd imagined, but surprisingly, he didn't close up on her.

"I like being my own boss. I make my own decisions, my own hours. If I have to go out of town for a few days, I just put a sign in the window, lock up and take off. And I enjoy dealing directly with people. Running a small establishment makes me happy."

"That's important," Sydney said knowingly. "Some people never figure out what they want to do."

"I had a lot of different jobs in my youth, so I made an educated decision about where I was headed," Benno told her. "I opened my first business in the L.A. area, and when that panned out, I came back here to open a second. Benno's Place is kind of a throwback to the early seventies—part pub, part coffeehouse—but it suits me."

She thought so, too. Before she could urge him on to new revelations, the delicate connection was broken.

"You through with those?" The kid from behind the counter was pointing to their plates.

"Yeah, I'm done," Benno said.

Sydney indicated he should clear hers away, as well. Sensing the moment of sharing had passed, she gathered the cards and stuffed them into their pouch.

"I guess we should continue our manhunt," Benno said, rising.

And they would continue their conversation later, Sydney thought with determination.

They methodically combed the streets for establishments with video games and pinball machines, checking tokens at each business. None were stamped with impressions of a seagull and boardwalk.

As they continued on, Benno couldn't help thinking about the incident in the hot dog joint. Would any tarot reader have seen so much in the cards or had Sydney's psychic powers jump-started her imagination? He had to admit she'd been right on target. How could she have been so certain about his past?

He should have opened up to her as she'd encouraged him to do. The only people he'd ever really talked to about the tragedy that had prompted him to leave town were Kenneth and Poppy. Plenty of people like

Parnell Anderson were ready to make judgments and impose them arbitrarily. They didn't forget and they certainly didn't forgive.

Why should they, when he hadn't forgiven himself?

But now, he'd been tempted to share himself fully with someone for the first time and he couldn't quite say why.

Maybe because he owed her.

Maybe his reasons were more complex.

Benno was unable to deny his growing attraction to Sydney Raferty. He'd thought that affinity was inappropriate when he believed she'd been Kenneth's wife. But she hadn't been married to his friend, hadn't been married at all. Still, she'd thought herself in love and Benno saw his own interest in Sydney as an intrusion of sorts. She had enough emotional baggage to handle without adding his to her load.

Barely a block from the larger Fun Zone area, they entered a medium-size game arcade called Mariner Amusements.

Benno told himself to remember his purpose—to help Sydney. The thing he feared most was that her involvement in the murder was his fault. His and, to a lesser degree, Kenneth's. Since a dead man couldn't be expected to assist anyone unless he could cross over from the grave, her welfare was in his hands.

And if he was responsible for getting Sydney into this mess, albeit in an indirect way, she would be glad to see the last of him. So maybe he would be wise to keep his own counsel for as long as possible.

Benno gave the place a once-over as they passed several kids playing video games. A teenager had just lost his ball on a double-decked pinball machine.

When the digital readout showed a score of one million, two hundred thousand, he slapped the machine's side in disgust. The half-dozen tokens lined up in a perfect row on the glass top jumped.

"Hey, buddy, can I check one of those out for a minute?" Benno asked.

"Huh?" The kid gave him a suspicious look, then nodded. "I guess so."

Picking up a token, Benno was aware that the teenager's eyes never left him. He smiled and turned the token so Sydney could see.

"A seagull . . . and a boardwalk!"

"Bingo." He set the coin back in place. "Thanks."

"This is it." Excitement colored Sydney's cheeks as well as her voice. "Now if only we can find someone who remembers our mystery man."

Benno placed an encouraging arm around her shoulders. Sydney rewarded him with a smile. As they stopped one of the employees who exchanged tokens for cash, he hoped that particular expression would stay put, that Sydney wouldn't be disappointed yet again. He was afraid exactly that would happen when, after she described the man she'd married, the token changers' face remained a blank.

"I coulda seen the guy, but I ain't sure."

"Try to remember," Sydney urged, but the employee merely shrugged.

"I think I know who you mean." This response came from a pretty blonde of about eighteen who was emptying one of the video games of tokens. Closing the door and straightening, she said, "This guy has kind of a crooked smile, right?"

"Right," Sydney croaked, moving toward the blonde. "And he smokes those thin brown cigarettes."

The blonde nodded. "The Fox. The girls all call him that 'cause of his dynamite looks."

"What's his real name?" Benno asked.

She shrugged and gave him the real once-over. Her smile told him she liked what she saw. "Never heard him called anything else. He used to hang out here a lot, but I haven't seen him in weeks. Said he was going on vacation, but I guess he's not back yet."

Or he was too busy making trouble for other people to hang around a game arcade, Benno thought. "Do you know if this Fox lives somewhere near here?"

"Carol, a customer up front needs help with one of the machines," a man in his thirties said. A tag on his white shirt identified him as the manager.

"Sure Mr. Vita." Flashing Benno a look of regret, the blonde hurried off.

The manager swept over each of them in turn, his weasel eyes not missing a detail. "Can I help you folks with something?"

Sydney's lips curved into a charming smile. "We're trying to find a man called The Fox."

"Doesn't ring a bell."

His tone of voice didn't ring true. Benno wondered if the manager was protecting a friend. And when Sydney repeated her description, he wondered where her intuition was, no less her psychic powers. Couldn't she tell the manager wasn't being straight with them? Then again, perhaps she wasn't fooled, either. She was carefully watching the guy for his reaction.

"Sorry. We get thousands of customers every week. Only someone with a photographic memory would be able to place any particular one."

"Thanks for your help."

Benno didn't miss the sarcasm in Sydney's voice. She held herself stiffly and walked toward the front of the arcade.

Carol had finished with the customer. As they passed her, she kept her back toward her boss and whispered, "The Fox and Mr. Vita are friendly, you know? I once heard him say something about meeting at Oceanview Apartments. Or was it Ocean Winds? Something with water in the name."

"Thanks," Sydney returned just as softly. Outside, she said, "I guess we look for a telephone directory again."

"You really think Fox is listed?"

"Probably not. But we can check for apartment complexes in the yellow pages."

She was correct. They had an assortment from which to choose: Oceanview, Ocean Winds, Seascape, Sea Breeze and Watersprite. And the various complexes seemed to be located within a half-mile radius of the arcade.

They started with the closest, Ocean Winds, where they were lucky enough to spot a tenant carrying groceries from a car. Sydney described the fake Kenneth, but the woman insisted no one by that description lived there.

Next they stopped at Watersprite, only to find it was a retirement community.

Ocean Winds was an exclusive enclave. The guard at the gate turned them away without answering any of their questions, which left that place a big question mark.

Only two places left to check.

Sea Breeze was the closest, several blocks inland. How it had gotten its name Benno couldn't fathom, since the water wasn't even visible from the complex,

"No one around," Sydney said dispiritedly.

"We could knock at doors."

"Or check mailboxes—not that it'll do us any good since we don't know The Fox's real name."

Benno tried to be encouraging. "We're here, aren't we?"

The building was small. Only a dozen tenants. And checking the mailboxes proved to be the smart thing to do.

"My God, Fox is his name!" An excited Sydney tapped the identification. "Al Fox. 2-F."

The two story building was old but in decent shape. An outside staircase led to a second-story landing that fronted the half-dozen apartments. Fox's was the farthest from the stairs. As they traversed the landing, Benno noted each apartment had a large picture window with smaller windows on each side. Some were curtained for privacy, others not.

Al Fox's were.

Benno rapped on the door. When he got no response, he banged harder. "Delivery for Mr. Al Fox."

Tension seemed to ooze from Sydney as they waited.

"He's not here," she said softly, her tone ripe with disappointment.

"Then we'll have to go in and take a look for ourselves."

"Break in?" she asked. "That's illegal."

Sometimes Sydney could be incredibly naive, but Benno guessed that was part of her charm.

"Do you want legal?" he asked. "Or do you want to find out why you may be indicted for murder?"

Chapter Nine

Wiping her sweaty palms on her white pants, Sydney stood guard as Benno proceeded with breaking in, his confidence making her wonder about his past yet again. Narrow screened windows flanked either side of the large bay. He stood in front of the one that had been left slightly open.

She wished he would hurry.

They'd spent the entire afternoon tracking down Fox and now people with day jobs were leaving work. She noted the increased foot traffic on the adjoining street. At any moment, a tenant from one of the other five second-story apartments was bound to come home and catch them.

The sound of tearing fiberglass sent gooseflesh down her back. She glanced in Benno's direction as he finished slicing through the entire length of screen. He folded his knife and stuck it into his pocket, deftly rolled up the fiberglass, then slid open the window and threw the evidence of the break-in inside.

"Ladies first."

Not at all comfortable with what they were doing, she checked the downstairs area thoroughly for any witnesses before edging back toward him. Benno had laughed when she'd suggested having the owner or manager open up the place for them. He'd said they wouldn't get into the apartment without a court order; they would only get in if they made the opportunity for themselves.

"Relax," he ordered. "No one's around. All you have to do is slip into the apartment and unlock the front door for me."

Sydney ignored her foreboding and gathered what measly courage she had left. Pulling aside the heavy orange drape that blocked the window, she took one last cursory look around outside. No one. And inside, nothing out of place except the rolled screen.

"Do you want me to do it?" Benno asked, his tone impatient.

Though Sydney would have loved to say yes, she decided not to. After all, he was setting himself up for possible trouble because he was helping her find a con man. And if they didn't find Fox, *she* would be in big trouble with the law. She couldn't let Benno take all the risks.

"I'm smaller. It'll be easier for me."

Benno steadied Sydney as she swung a leg over the sill. His hands were warm and his grip firm on her sides. The situation evoked memories of other hands on her flesh.

Al Fox's hands.

A felon's hands.

Shifting her weight away from Benno as she stepped inside brought a measure of relief even though she didn't relish being in the room alone. Her pulse racing, she rushed to the door and flung it open.

Benno gave her a questioning look as he stepped inside and closed the door behind him. Sydney figured her fear was written all over her face. But she wasn't a coward; she was merely out of her depth. And she couldn't help wondering what fate had in store for her next.

"I've never done anything like this before," she told him.

Sydney noticed Benno didn't add his assurance that neither had he. But then his attention was off her and on the room itself.

"What a drab setting for a man who sounds like a peacock," he commented.

She bristled for a moment, then realized she had no reason to defend the man who'd tricked her into a fake marriage. Taking a good look around, she was somewhat shocked by the lack of amenities and the excess of filth. The room was sparsely decorated, the few pieces of furniture obviously secondhand and in need of cleaning. The room's musty smell seemed appropriate to the setting.

Benno wandered toward the kitchenette. The small table was covered with food wrappers, and several bags from fast-food restaurants lay crumpled on the floor.

"He must have had lunch here." Benno picked up a container. "I can still smell the greasy fries."

"Then he may be back at any minute."

Panic collided with excitement at the possibility of confronting Al Fox. Of course that's exactly what she'd been hoping for. Only caution dictated she not be so anxious—the man was probably armed.

"Odds are our Mr. Vita warned him," Benno said. "Fox is probably long gone and I don't picture him coming back. He can't be sure you won't call the police and have the building staked out. His hideaway isn't safe anymore.''

"Just in case you're wrong, we'd better search the apartment fast and see what we can find."

Benno was already opening a door. "This closet is empty."

"You look around here. I'll check the bedroom."

It was as sordid as the rest of the place, making Sydney wonder how Al Fox could have fooled her so well. His taste had seemed impeccable and when he was with her, he'd seemed something of a perfectionist. She couldn't fathom how any human being could live in such squalor. More wrappers littered the dresser, half a doughnut lay on the nightstand next to an ashtray filled with cigarette butts, and what appeared to be several days worth of newspapers were scattered across the floor.

"Fox was one hell of an actor, I'll give him that," she muttered, dropping her shoulder bag at the edge of his bed.

She started with the chest. Either other clothes had been hastily ripped from the drawers before he'd left, or Fox had had only these few things and didn't care how wrinkled they were. She found nothing more revealing.

Though she expected the closet to be empty, she checked it next. There were only a few hangers holding articles of clothing, all of which she recognized. He'd left them as if he wanted no reminder of her.

Sadness threatened to overwhelm her, but Sydney steeled herself, ordered herself to remain detached. She inspected the clothes, searched through pockets, including those of a heavy sweater he'd worn the day he'd proposed. Nothing. Touching the sweater sleeve, she closed her eyes and visualized the man she'd fallen in love with.

She'd just said yes to his proposal and he was holding her and wearing that devastatingly crooked smile....

His face neared hers to claim a kiss....

She shuddered at the memory.

Then a hand on her shoulder made her jump. Her eyes flew open. "Benno!"

"Hey, are you okay?"

"Just a little jittery," she lied, swinging out of the closet and trying to pass him.

His hand shot out, preventing her from going any farther. Benno pulled her against his chest and wrapped both arms around her as if to stop her trembling. Sydney pressed her cheek against the front of his soft brown shirt. His heart beat strongly and steadily beneath the finely woven material. Being held by him—leaning on him both literally and figuratively—felt so right.

And only a few hours before, she had thought she was unwilling to get close to any man.

"Better?"

Wondering how she could feel so content in his arms, especially in this place, especially with the memories she'd conjured, Sydney lifted her head to meet his gaze.

"Much."

He was staring at her in a way that mesmerized her. She told herself she should pull away from him, but she couldn't move. Didn't want to move. His expression intense, Benno lowered his head as she had remembered Al Fox doing. She forced away the recollection and lifted her face.

Benno's mouth demanded hers. Sydney let loose the emotions she'd been trying to deny. For days, she'd fought her attraction to this man and yet should have known that some physical exploration was inevitable. She responded as if she hadn't been held in years, as if the embrace was evidence of her own desirability.

Evidence that she desperately needed.

And Benno's kiss was more wonderful than she could have imagined. She felt intrigued. She felt plundered. She felt alive.

She was so caught up in the wonder of Benno's embrace that she didn't realize they weren't alone until a strident female voice demanded, "What in blue blazes is going on here?"

Sydney jumped and pushed at Benno's chest. Caught red-handed. She was ready to confess everything and plead for the woman's mercy.

Benno, on the other hand, kept his head . . . and an arm around Sydney.

He gave her a warning squeeze before asking the woman, "And who might you be?"

Fiftyish, reed thin and wearing hot-pink shorts, a lime-green halter top, and several colorful necklaces and bracelets, and a pair of earrings that resembled miniature chandeliers, the brassy redhead drew herself up to her full height.

"I'm the one doing the asking around here. Ida Mae Sims. This is my building."

"And you always come waltzing into your tenants' apartments without being invited?" Benno challenged her.

Sydney gave him an exasperated look. Why wasn't he trying to charm the woman?

"You aren't my tenants," Ida Mae said, jingling her rhinestone-decorated key ring at him.

"No, but Al Fox is. We're waiting for him."

The landlady's mouth puckered, giving her narrow face a pinched look. "Is that no-good scoundrel gonna be here soon? I thought you was him. That's why I came up here—to collect the rent. He's good at giving me a song and dance instead of hard cash." She narrowed her heavily made-up eyes suspiciously. "And how do I know you're his friends?"

"How else would we have gotten into this place if he didn't let us in?" Benno asked smoothly while Sydney prayed the landlady hadn't noticed the screen.

"I don't know, but I want you outta here."

"That won't make Al happy."

"Tough. When he makes me happy by putting a rent check in my hand—" she tapped one palm with long purple nails "—then everything will be ducky. You tell him that when you see him. In the meantime, I'm gonna get my gentleman friend to change the lock."

"We can wait right here and give Al your message," Sydney said. To appease the woman, she added, "I'm sure he'll want to square things with you."

"Well, I ain't sure of no such thing, so you two get out of here right this dang minute."

She waltzed around behind them and herded them out of the bedroom. They were through the front door before Sydney remembered her shoulder bag.

"My purse. I left it in the bedroom."

Ida Mae sighed and fussed with the magenta silk flowers in her hair. "All right. Go in and get it."

Sydney gave the landlady a grateful smile and reentered the apartment. She headed for the bedroom and wondered if she could stall long enough to check out the other dresser. Before picking up her purse, she peered through the doorway to see if Ida Mae was watching.

"Hurry up now!"

The voice jarred Sydney and she knocked into the shoulder bag, which tumbled off the bed. Its contents shot across the floor.

"Damn."

Bending over, she grabbed her wallet, keys and lipstick and dumped them back into her purse. But when she went for the tarot pouch, the opening loosened and several cards slid out and flew under the bed.

Now she had to get on her knees and the floor was filthy. She collected the first few cards easily but had to flatten out to reach two others that had landed on a piece of paper almost out of reach. She nabbed the edge and dragged it and the cards toward her. Sitting back on her knees, she brushed the dust from the front of her sea-green shirt.

Then she reached for the cards. They rested on a newspaper clipping, yellowed and fragile, with deep creases where it had been folded, perhaps for years. Curiosity made her pick it up. When she turned the clipping over, her eyes widened.

"What's the doggone problem?" Ida Mae stood in the doorway, hands on her hips.

"I—I knocked over my purse," Sydney croaked, carefully folding up the newspaper and putting it into her purse. "I was just picking up my things."

The other woman came closer. "Tarot cards. You read them?"

"Yes."

"I love tarot cards!" Ida Mae chirped enthusiastically. "Would you read mine? I'll pay."

Sweeping the loose cards into her bag, Sydney stood and rushed by the other woman. "No, sorry, I don't have time."

"I see." Ida Mae yelled after her. "You have time enough for your boyfriend but not for an honest, hardworking woman who could use a little advice about her future well-being. So much for the sisterhood!"

Her heart pounding, Sydney caught up with Benno who had wandered a short way down the landing. "Let's get out of here."

"Calm down, we're fine."

"You may be." She kept going. "I need a drink."

"You remember what I told you now!" Ida Mae yelled after them.

Sydney didn't look back. Her mind was racing as fast as her feet as she descended the stairs. She and Benno had come to the conclusion that she was an innocent pawn in the game of murder, chosen merely because she'd been at a low point and vulnerable. Now she knew that theory was wrong.

As if to reflect her charged emotions, the sky had darkened prematurely. Dull and gray, it threatened rain. If only a storm could wash away the panic she was feeling.

Benno caught up to her as she reached street level. "So what did Ida Mae tell you?"

"Nothing. She must have wanted us to remind Al Fox about the rent money."

"Then why are you so upset?" he persisted. "Because we got caught or because we didn't find anything? We could go back later to finish the job."

"No. We don't have to. I already found more than I wanted."

"While you were getting your purse?"

Sydney nodded. How ironic. If she hadn't gone back into the bedroom, she would still be operating on an incorrect premise.

"Let's find a place to sit down and I'll show you."

Despite the late hour, throngs of people crowded the streets. She would have thought they'd be home or at some restaurant eating dinner. When they entered the nearest bar called The Puffin, it was surprisingly empty. Claiming a quiet corner, Benno ordered a beer, Sydney a gin and tonic. She could use the gin straight, but she also wanted a clear head. While she needed something to calm her nerves, she still had to be in charge of her faculties.

"All right," Benno said after the waitress left to fill their order. "What's the big secret you discovered?"

"It's not exactly a secret, merely something I wish I didn't have to face." Rather than show him the clipping immediately, she decided to give him some background. "Several years ago, I was in charge of a successful ad campaign for *Flawless*. That's a line of competitively priced hair products and makeup aimed at the professional woman."

"I'm familiar with the name."

"Part of the campaign's success was a result of the popularity of the model-actress I chose to be our spokeswoman. You remember her—Honor Bright." When Benno shook his head and shrugged, she retrieved the clipping from her bag. "Maybe you'll recognize her then. Honor and I were out celebrating when this picture was taken. The next morning, it appeared in *Variety*."

Her fingers trembled as she smoothed out the newspaper clipping on top of the table. The photograph of her and Honor dominated the piece.

Benno looked as shocked as she'd felt when she'd first seen the clipping.

"So you found this in Fox's bedroom," he murmured.

"Proving that we've been deluding ourselves," she went on. "Fox wouldn't have had this in his possession unless I was his intended victim."

A GREEN PONTIAC SAT PARKED across from The Puf fin, its driver hunched low in the seat behind the wheel.

The winds had picked up and rain was imminent. Good. DeMartino and the Raferty woman would be more concerned with the weather than with someone following them.

Sydney Raferty had complicated matters when she'd latched on to Benno DeMartino.

He didn't like complications.

Now his plans would have to be changed. Again. Things had been going awry every time he turned around. He'd stuck Kenneth Lord away, had been keeping him alive for insurance until he was sure he had her. But the prisoner had escaped. Too bad for Lord. If only he would have stayed put instead of trying that stupid stunt, he might have lived a while longer.

If only *he'd* gotten rid of the body, the man chided himself, everything would be jake. But he'd figured he didn't have time with Martha waiting. His mistake. Recognizing his slipup after the fact did him no good whatsoever.

The first drops of rain splattered the car as he contemplated how much he hated things going wrong. So messy. He couldn't afford to let things get any further out of hand.

This was one mess he was about to straighten out at the first opportunity.

WIPERS SLAPPED AT the shower flooding the windshield. Waiting for the weather to clear had been a waste of time. The rain was coming in fits and spurts, not enough to flood the road but enough to be annoying. Benno figured they should have headed back to Stone Beach instead of having that drink. They'd nursed them for a half hour in hopes that the storm would blow over. In the end, he'd had to call Poppy to ask her to open up the coffeehouse. Now the sky had gone from gray to near black and fog was rising from the soaked ground.

"Why should an absolute stranger be out to destroy me?" Sydney was muttering again as if he was supposed to come up with the answer. "Why would he marry me and why use Kenneth Lord's name and then kill him?"

They'd mulled over the situation since she'd shown him the clipping, but they had come to no logical conclusions. It was hard to pin a motive on a stranger.

"Maybe you were both intended to be victims," Benno offered, though that sounded pretty lame even to him. The situation was too puzzling. He should suggest hiring a top detective.

"But what could I possibly have done to make myself the target of someone's sick desire for revenge?"

"The ad campaign?" That was a natural guess based on the newspaper clipping. "Maybe Fox isn't exactly a stranger. What if he was a competitor and you stole his account and ruined his reputation or made him go broke?"

She shook her head. "*Flawless* was a new product line. We'd had the parent company's account forever. I can't believe a ticked off ad exec would go to this extreme over losing an account. Besides, that was what—three years ago?"

"I've heard you have to be crazy to be in advertising." Realizing he was clumping Sydney in with the rest, he said, "Uh, sorry, no offense."

"No offense taken."

Benno wondered what she was thinking when she took refuge in silence and stared out the side window. The road to Stone Beach was a two-laner except for the exit approaches where it broadened for a short stretch. And it wound along the coast, normally giving an occasional glimpse of beach and sea. But not tonight. Benno flicked on his brights to cut through the dense fog. Glancing up into his rear-view mirror, he noticed the car behind him had done the same.

He averted his eyes from the mirror. He would have to concentrate if he wanted to stay on the road.

But his mind wasn't cooperating—it kept straying back to the question: Who other than a crazy person would have kept that clipping for years? Visualizing the photo, he thought about the stunning actress who'd posed with Sydney.

"What about Honor Bright?" Benno asked. "Maybe something strange has been happening to her, too. I don't remember seeing her face lately."

"She's not in the mainstream anymore," Sydney told him. "She's living in Seattle, acting as spokesperson for the salmon industry. I gave her a lead on the job about a year ago. She sent me a thank-you card, but we haven't been in touch since. I guess I could find her if I tried."

Though Honor wasn't a likely lead, Benno thought. Still, they couldn't afford to let anything slip by them. Finding the newspaper clipping had blown a hole through his theory that the revenge had been aimed at him, that Parnell Anderson had been responsible. Thank God.

When they got Sydney free of this mess, she wouldn't have that as a reason to turn away from him.

He didn't want to give her any reason, Benno thought, remembering the kiss. Sydney had probably turned to him out of distress, to be comforted, but he'd had different reasons.

He was falling for Sydney and couldn't quite say why. What put her above other women he'd been interested in over the past several years, many more beautiful and self-possessed than she? He hadn't even known her long enough to form a relationship. He could only think their common experience—running away from a painful background—was now drawing them together. Not that their circumstances had been in the least similar. He could hardly compare his hand-to-mouth existence with that of a judge's daughter. Yet as surely as he had left his past behind, so had Sydney.

But now both their pasts were confronting them.

Brights flicking in his rearview mirror caught Benno's attention. The driver behind him wanted to pass, and they were on an extended curve. Noting an advance sign indicating the exit to the state park was just ahead, he turned on his signal. He'd pull over to the right where the road widened.

But before he could do so, the other car picked up speed, the brights looming large in his mirror.

He squinted to protect his vision. "Damn fool, give me a minute."

Sydney stirred in her seat. "What's going on?"

Benno speeded up. "Road hog in a hurry." The road widened and he pulled to the right.

The other car did the same.

Aggravated, Benno pulled back to the left. The lights in the mirror followed. Either some jerk was playing games or...

"I think we're being followed."

"What?" Sydney turned in her seat to see. "My God, he's so close."

Even as she said the words, Benno swerved to the right barely in time to make the exit; the other car stayed on his tail.

He thought quickly. The entrance to the state park north of town was directly ahead. A road wound uphill, eventually splitting, the right fork going to an overlook, the left fork joining a lower road skirting the beach. He didn't like his choices, but stopping in the middle of nowhere to face an unknown, possibly armed pursuer wasn't an option he was willing to consider.

"Hold on," he said grimly. "I'm going to try to lose him."

"It's Fox, isn't it?"

Benno didn't answer, merely stepped on the gas and shot into the state park. He was trying to get a good lead on the other car before getting to the fork. Maybe he could elude Al Fox or whoever it was that was following them.

The incline dropped off steeply on either side. While the rain had stopped, the fog had thickened to the consistency of a gray-white soup. He was nearly driving blind and hoped that nothing—or no one—would suddenly appear on the road or they would all be goners.

His plan was working. Slowly but surely, the other car was falling behind.

Hoping memory would serve him well, Benno stepped on the gas halfway through a hairpin curve and pulled the wheel sharply to the left. The next curve was gentler and to the right. They were approaching the fork, and for the moment, the lights of the other car had disappeared altogether.

"He's gone," Sydney said with a sigh of relief.

"Don't fool yourself. He's only slowed down because he doesn't know the road." Benno took the left fork and they began a gentler sweeping descent. "Let's hope he guesses wrong and heads for the overlook."

"You seem to know this road well enough to drive it in your sleep."

Benno didn't think there was any harm in telling her why. "When I was in high school, we used to use these roads as a racecourse till the cops caught us once too often."

"So you were a wild one."

A confirmation rather than a question. If only she knew how wild, she might not be sitting next to him. Not that he was proud of the fact. That was part of the reason he'd avoided telling her about his past. But evasion was hard work. He knew he couldn't maintain his "good guy" camouflage forever.

"Benno, he guessed right. I see his lights."

Checking his rearview mirror, Benno cursed softly. "Damn!"

He'd inadvertently let up on the accelerator when he should have increased his speed. This stretch of the road was easier to negotiate, but when they reached the bottom of the incline, only one route remained that might allow him to lose the other car. He had no choice.

"We're going to have to cross the beach."

"In this fog?"

"Do you have a better idea?"

She didn't answer, and continued to watch out the back window as he turned the Thunderbird onto a road separated from the sand by a concrete retaining wall.

Though driving a car on this end of the beach was legal—as was true among most of Oregon's coastline—the stretch fronting the town limits was an exception. In addition, bringing a car that far south was dangerous. The unrelenting ocean had broken off chunks of seastacks over the years, depositing the boulders near the water's edge.

"He's gaining on us," Sydney told him as they approached a break in the retaining wall.

"Hold on."

Praying his car would make it, Benno swerved onto the beach. Now if only it hadn't rained enough to turn the sand into a shifting morass. The Thunderbird flew over the two-foot drop and landed with a teeth-jarring jolt. Benno let his foot off the accelerator. The tires bit into the wet sand and found traction. He didn't dare go too fast lest the spinning wheels dig them into an early grave.

Now if only the driver would be less cautious. . . .

But the lights in the mirror told him the other man was taking his lead and following carefully. Eventually, they would run out of beach. Then what? There was no other road at the sound end—only cliff. They would have to abandon the car and make a run for it when they neared the center of town.

Resolved to get them to safety, Benno edged his speed more than made him comfortable.

He glanced at Sydney to see how she was doing.

One hand clutched the dash for support as she kept silent watch; she seemed to be holding up well. He faced forward, but the seconds of diverted attention proved long enough for potential disaster. Before them lay a yellow hulk—an abandoned beach trike. He braked and swerved, but hit the trike a glancing blow.

The Thunderbird's wheels dug into the sand and began to spin.

"Get out," he yelled at Sydney, even as he cut the engine and lights. "We have to run for it." He opened his door and flew out of the car. Seeing that Sydney was struggling with her purse, he swore. "Leave the damn thing!"

"No! The evidence." With a jerk, she pulled the bag free. Slamming the door, she hurried to the front of the car. "Which way?"

Benno grabbed her hand and flinched at the screech of brakes behind them.

"Come on, run!"

He practically jerked her arm out of its socket and pulled her off her feet before she found the power to keep up with him. If only he could see something, be able to identify exactly where they were. They were running blind.

Suddenly, a shot pierced the night.

"Oh, God," Sydney sobbed. "He does have a gun."

Another gunshot made Benno lurch to the side—pain, hot and searing, numbed his arm.

Chapter Ten

Benno almost knocked Sydney over as he stumbled against her.

"Oh, my God, you've been hit!" she cried, trying to support him with her own light weight.

Not that a bullet was enough to stop him. He righted himself, and, his grip even tighter now, continued to drag her forward until he jerked to a halt with a muttered curse.

"Careful," he said softly. "Rocks."

He slowed accordingly and veered to the right. Toward the sea. Sydney could hear the ocean's curl as a wave slapped the shoreline. Though the fog was thick, she knew they were close to the water's edge.

"Benno—"

Her protest cut off by a squeeze that practically numbed her hand, she allowed him to lead her over pebble-strewn sand that eventually gave way to more solid stone. He slowed some, yet seemed to know exactly where he was going. Surely their attacker wouldn't be foolish enough to follow blindly.

"You don't have a flashlight in that monstrosity you call a purse, do you?" he whispered.

"As a matter of fact . . ."

They stopped. Sydney felt for her key ring, attached to which was a pencil-sized flashlight. Pulling the ring from the purse, she found and flicked on the thin beam which shone weakly, a ribbon softening the fog for a few yards. Even its modest light would help keep them safe. She lifted the shoulder strap and hooked the bag over her head and under one arm so she'd have both hands free.

They continued on, Benno leading her straight toward the sea.

Another breaker rolled in, soaking Sydney's feet and ankles. Luckily, she was wearing canvas shoes with rubber soles that kept her fairly steady on the slippery rock. Benno slowed his stride to accommodate the rising water. Now it surged, engulfing her knees, slapping against her thighs, splashing her chest. The current eddied and sucked around her, as if trying to drag her away from Benno.

He held on tighter.

Remembering the dream in which she had drowned, Sydney felt panic rise in her throat. "Benno." When he didn't answer, she jerked on his arm before remembering he'd been hit.

He moaned. "Ahh! What did you do that for?"

"Sorry. It's just the water—my dream."

"Trust me," he grunted softly, through what sounded like clenched teeth.

When she heard muffled curses, Sydney surveyed the area behind them. A lightened area in the fog some distance away made her realize they were still being stalked and their pursuer had a flashlight of his own. A *big* flashlight whose beam could easily pin them if they didn't hurry and find a place to hide. Despite her fear of the ocean, she allowed Benno to lead her farther out into deeper water. Foam rushed over her hips and licked the channel between her breasts.

She took a steadying breath, clenched her jaw and said nothing.

When she was certain she couldn't tolerate going any farther, the water began to recede and the footing became surer. They traveled over solid rock, the base of a seastack, which rose in a gentle incline. Benno squeezed her hand encouragingly. Clambering over and skirting boulders, they climbed inexorably higher and higher until they reached a shelf that narrowed to the left.

"Hug the rockface," Benno instructed as he went first. "And move with me. Carefully."

She followed him, all the while praying neither of them would lose their footing. Progress was slow but steady until they came to an area with a wider lip.

"We're almost there," he assured her. "We'll.have to climb up about six feet or so."

"Blind?"

"Do you want him to find us?"

Fear countered her good sense. "All right. Where?"

Benno took the flashlight and showed her. Nerves taut, Sydney began the tortuous ascent, his hand pressed to the middle of her back, steadying her. Somehow, he followed with ease, though he had only one good arm that he was using to help her. She was having trouble making it with two.

A moment later, she almost panicked. "I can't find any footing."

Directly behind her, he flashed the light over the slick surface, stopping when the beam picked up a rocky protrusion. Her mouth went dry at the thought of her weight dislodging the tiny ledge, her body following the stone, to be sucked up by the greedy waters below.

Hand flattened against her backside, Benno urged her on. "Up and over a few feet to the left," he whispered, flashing the light so she could see what appeared to be an opening between the boulders.

Praying, Sydney did as instructed, and only when she landed on the larger flat area in front of the entrance to a cave did she remember to breathe.

Then Benno was next to her, an arm across her back, pushing her into a crouched position.

"Here, take the flashlight. Watch your head and go into the cave."

"What if it's not empty?"

"You won't find anything too horrible inside. On the other hand, something horrible is waiting for you out here."

Scouring the area before her with the light, Sydney found it free of unwelcome creatures. She braved the narrow mouth of the tunnel, stopping a few yards inside where she could stand upright. Something brushed her hair. She would have screamed if Benno hadn't covered her mouth with his hand. Her light caught a fluttering bird, one of several taking shelter from the storm. Outside, splashing sounds made by human feet rather than by an incoming wave pinpointed their pursuer as being within spitting distance.

Shooting distance, Sydney corrected herself.

The wait seemed interminable, but Benno pressed her into the damp cold wall, his hand eventually moving from her mouth to the side of her arm.

Sydney tried to relax, but between the danger outside and the danger within, she felt trapped.

Benno was so close... too close.

Five minutes went by.

Her nerves were ready to explode. Her skin felt seared where Benno touched her. His muscles were coiled, ready to spring him into action, while her breathing became shallow, her heartbeat irregular.

Ten minutes.

The danger had heightened her senses, had removed the thin veil of pretense she'd kept between them. Benno stirred against her, obviously as uncomfortable as she, and yet he did not speak. She sensed he was focused on listening for any change in sound outside their shelter. She tried to focus as well, but memories of the kiss he'd taken from her earlier prompted all kinds of romantic thoughts.

Thoughts she didn't want to own up to.

Maybe twenty minutes, she thought. Enough!

"Surely he's gone by now," Sydney finally said. "We can take a look."

But when they returned to the cave's entrance, she realized the weather had worsened. Rain pounded rock. And the rush of the sea sounded closer as a wave broke with tremendous force against the seastack, spraying them both not only with water but with tiny stones. Sydney raised a hand to protect her face.

"The tide is almost fully in," Benno told her. "We'll have to wait."

"For what? To be drowned?"

"The water won't rise this high."

"How do you know?"

"I've spent the night in this cave before," he admitted. "More than once."

"Recently?"

"Years ago."

"Things could have changed."

Sydney was bent on extricating herself from this situation as quickly as possible. She had no intention of spending the night in close quarters with Benno DeMartino. He was too tempting.

And from recent experience, Sydney knew she was too weak to resist.

She started to inch away from him. "I'm going to leave while I can."

"No." He caught her around the waist and dragged her backward.

"Benno!" Though Sydney struggled valiantly, she was but a fly against his strength as he drew her back into the shelter of the tunnel and to the raised area they'd just left. "We could drown in here."

"You'd drown out there for sure." He sounded angry with her. "I know what I'm talking about. Trying to get back to shore in the fog and rain would be a dumb move at any time."

"We made it up here."

"We were lucky, and we didn't have a choice. But we have a choice now. And we've got high tide to boot. We'll be safe inside the cave. Trust me."

"I do trust you, though heaven knows why. You're a walking mystery." Afraid of more than the gunman who'd undoubtedly given up the search, Sydney was trying to start a fight, to give herself a reason to leave, to keep her emotions safe. "I don't know the first thing about you. Every time I try to figure you out a little, you put me off."

"Maybe it's time I told you about myself."

"Oh, right."

"If that's what it'll take to keep you safe, I'll talk until the tide goes back out."

He sounded sincere enough. And concerned. Sydney weakened. She would stay if for no other reason than to find out more about her mysterious dark knight.

As if he realized she'd capitulated, he let go but took the flashlight from her. "Come on, there's a larger chamber farther inside."

Using the beam to show her another low opening, he indicated she should proceed him. Not about to enter the dark now that there was no urgency, she took back the flashlight and shone it on the rocky walls of a larger chamber. Birds resting in nooks and crannies watched them. A few flitted across the cave as if frightened by the intrusion.

"Seems safe enough. Where are we, anyway?" she asked, practically getting to her knees to scoot inside.

"In the heart of The Sugar Loaf."

She inspected the area as best she could. The remainder of a fire at one end had been drenched by water seeping down the wall from an opening that would act as a chimney and draw out the smoke on a dry night.

"How did you know about this cave?"

"A misspent youth."

He didn't sound as if he was joking. He sounded strange, actually, as if his memories were anything but positive. She wondered what had happened in this place to make him so tense.

"Too bad we can't build a fire," Benno said ruefully. "At least the place is mostly dry."

But Sydney wasn't. Her clothes were soaked. Now that the urgency of the chase had died, she was aware of her physical discomfort. Cold seeped into her very bones as she sat as far away from the wet area as possible. Removing her shoulder bag, she threw the key ring and flashlight into the pouch and set it down next to her. She huddled, arms around her knees, but couldn't stop shivering.

Benno sprawled next to her, slipped an arm around her shoulders and pulled her close. Sydney would have protested but for his natural warmth that almost made her forget their wet garments.

"Better?"

"Mmm." Her shivering subsided. "So talk. I want to hear about that misspent youth of yours."

"You may be disillusioned."

"I have a fertile imagination. I was in advertising, remember? I may, in fact, be disappointed, instead."

"I'm not so sure about that. I was what my teachers called a hellion." He laughed, but the sound was bitter. "Actually, the entire town called me that or worse."

"Even your parents?"

Benno lapsed into a silence that made Sydney feel awkward. And his muscles coiled as they had earlier. Obviously, she'd struck a nerve.

"My mother ran out on us when I was five," he told her. "Pa and me. She just up and went. We never knew where. Or why for that matter. Pa said she'd always been restless and that she'd gone off in search of bright lights and fantasies. He promised she'd be back once she got it out of her system, but he was wrong."

Sydney was appalled. What kind of a mother would intentionally leave her child? She wished she could see his face, that he could see hers. Communicating in the dark was so unsatisfying. Yet, perhaps for him, the sense of anonymity made it easier to talk.

"You never heard from your mother again?"

"Never. Pa couldn't get over her leaving like that. First he made the excuses. Then he started drinking and losing jobs, one after another . . . stopped coming home some nights."

"He left you alone when you were five?"

"Seven. Maybe eight. I don't really remember," Benno told her. "By the time I was ten or so, Pa started disappearing for days, sometimes for weeks. That left me with a lot of time on my hands."

"Which you didn't use to your best advantage."

"You got that straight. I was angry, and I found ways to entertain myself—only other people didn't think I was so amusing."

Sydney remembered the references he'd made to knowing how to steal a car. And he'd had no difficulty in getting into Fox's apartment. He'd learned a lot more during his father's absences than merely fending for himself.

"So you got into fights?" she asked.

"Every kid gets into fights. I started them. I lied, cheated and stole. Getting caught didn't stop me."

"What did?"

Benno fell silent and she knew she'd struck another nerve. The anxiety gripping him was evident, even in the dark. His body told her what he wasn't saying in words.

Trying to lighten his mood, she asked, "So what's the dumbest thing you ever did?"

"Getting too close to the wrong person."

She sensed that had been the wrong question. "Someone who got you into trouble?"

"Not exactly. I was able to do that all on my own."

He was speaking obliquely and she was afraid he would resort to his old avoidance techniques if she pushed too far. She slid an arm across his chest in an effort to be comforting. He relaxed a bit and she decided to reroute the subject to a safer one.

"Does everyone in Stone Beach know about this cave?"

"Probably, though I'd wager not many people have actually been up here."

"I can relate to that. If I'd been able to see better, *I* probably wouldn't be in here. Facing a gun might have looked safer. Who showed you the entrance?"

"I found it on my own when I was twelve."

"You just woke up one morning and decided you were going to find the cave?"

"You could call it an act of desperation. The reason seems silly now."

Since she couldn't seem to hit on a safe topic, she decided to dive back in. "Having someone to talk to helps."

"So you've told me." He barely hesitated before going on. "I'd been hanging around the drugstore, reading magazines. I tried to steal them. The owner took after me and chased me down the street, yelling. He said I was worthless and warned me never to come back into his store again. Some of my classmates saw the episode and you can imagine their reaction."

"Children can be cruel," Sydney said, knowing firsthand exactly how cruel.

"I was furious. I hated the store owner, hated the town, hated Pa for leaving me alone. I was going to show them all by doing something they couldn't."

"By finding the cave on your own?" she asked.

"You got it. I had some stupid notion that I would be the first. I was going to make this cave my secret hideaway. And when the other kids found out, they'd all want to be my pals.''

Sydney felt a surge of compassion for the lonely, abandoned child he had been. But pity was the last thing a man like Benno could accept.

"How long did it take you to find the cave?"

"Several hours. There are a couple of places that look like entrances lower down. And I fell a couple of times. Actually, I split my chin open, but I didn't let a little blood stop me. I was pretty determined back then."

"Then? You're pretty determined to get what you want now."

He actually sounded as if he was amused when he said, "Some things never change."

"And others do?" she prompted.

"When I left this town, I bid it good riddance. I was certain I would never come back."

And Sydney was certain he hadn't told her everything. Something more than petty crimes on his part and petty meanness on the parts of the townspeople had made him leave. She hoped he would trust her enough to tell her about it.

"Why did you return?" she asked.

"The part of me that changed wouldn't have it any other way. I guess I felt I had to prove I could do anything I wanted."

Or that he was good enough, Sydney thought. Of course he was, always had been, but undoubtedly he had scars that ran deeper than the one on his chin, scars so deep they might never heal. She could only imagine what he must have gone through. And people like Martha Lord, Mick Brickman and that self-important Parnell Anderson wouldn't make his being accepted any easier.

"Helping me isn't going to help you," Sydney predicted.

"Maybe I don't care about being accepted as much as I thought I did."

She knew that was a lie. He cared, all right. She didn't need ESP to know that.

She'd been a misfit in her own way. She, too, had hidden from who she was. She'd started over, made a new life for herself in California, had even thought she was happy. But who could be satisfied living a lie, denying his own identity? That's what Benno seemed to have done, but he had the courage to face his past.

Would she ever be able to say the same for herself?

When silence stretched between them, she had the distinct feeling he was through talking about himself for one night. She could prompt him, remind him of his promise to talk about himself until the tide came in, threaten to run back out into the night. But that would make her as cruel as the people he had learned to hate.

Benno had shared so much of himself that she would have to be satisfied for now.

"You're so quiet," he said. "Did I succeed in disillusioning you?"

"Not at all. You'll have to tell me more some other time."

When he was ready, she thought.

He merely grunted in response, yet she sensed he was more open and relaxed with her than he had been since she'd known him. She, on the other hand, was anything but relaxed. Silence gave her too much time to consider her attraction. Perhaps if she moved away...

"Where do you think you're going?" he demanded when she tried.

"This can't be comfortable for you."

"Am I complaining?"

"Your arm must be going to sleep. Oh, God, your arm . . . the wound."

"It's the other arm," he said, chuckling.

"This isn't funny. Let me get the flashlight and look at it," she said, trying to move away again.

He pulled her back into his side. "My arm is fine. It's only a flesh wound, and the bleeding stopped long ago."

"The wound should be cleaned."

"No doubt the saltwater did the trick. My arm stung like hell."

"Benno!"

"Hush."

His mouth found hers in the dark as if drawn by a magnet. She'd been almost calm, settled, but now his lips stirred her deeply. As if his telling her about himself had freed her of self-imposed constraints, Sydney put all of herself into the embrace. This was only a kiss, she told herself. Surely no harm would come from a kiss.

And then she stopped thinking as his hand edged under her shirt and found her breast. He flicked the nipple, made it tighten, grasped the bud between thumb and forefinger and gently squeezed.

She moaned into his mouth.

Her palm drifted up his chest to his neck, memorizing every inch along the way. Her forefinger grazed the diamond earring as she slid her hand toward his damp hair. Several strands had come loose from where it was tied. She twined her fingers in it and smiled against his mouth, for a moment amused that she was kissing a man who had longer hair and was wearing more jewelry than she.

Then, when Benno caressed her, smoothed the flat of her stomach and slipped his hand between her thighs, the depth of her response sobered her.

She freed her mouth and tried to pull away.

Benno didn't let her go. "Sydney?"

"No, please."

She struggled fruitlessly. He held her pressed firmly to his side.

"At least let me hold you," he said. "We can keep each other warm through the night."

Sydney stopped fighting him. Wrapped in Benno's arms, she felt so right, so safe.

Safe from the villain who'd been stalking them, she realized, but not from memories. Especially not from the memory of how oblivious she'd been to Al Fox's true intentions. Even with her gifts, she hadn't been able to see beyond the surface. Blinded by what she'd thought was love, she'd allowed a stranger to seduce her both physically and mentally.

This time was different, she told herself.

How? an inner voice asked.

Because she wouldn't allow herself to get so deeply involved. She wasn't in love with Benno, she simply couldn't be. She'd married another man only a week before—or so she had thought. She could no longer trust her own emotions. Duped once, she had no intentions of deluding herself again. She couldn't get involved until she was whole again.

Guilt stole through Sydney as she realized she was being unfair to Benno. He hadn't sought her out. He'd been drawn into this mystery—into danger—because of her and out of loyalty to an old friend. He'd had no other reason to involve himself. She and Benno had merely been drawn together by an extraordinary situation.

When this was over, when Fox was caught and imprisoned, she would leave Stone Beach, would leave Benno, and try to put the pieces of her life back together. He would understand, she told herself. Though he hadn't yet told her why, he, too, had felt it necessary to leave Stone Beach and this had been his home.

Even as she rationalized, Benno hugged her closer, rubbed his cheek against her hair.

And Sydney felt an impending sense of loss she refused to define.

"I SHOULD ARREST the both of you," Brickman said when Benno and Sydney walked into his inner office at the police station.

"On what charges?" Benno asked.

Not in the best of moods, he wasn't about to put up with Brickman's garbage this early in the morning. It wasn't much after the crack of dawn and he hadn't slept well. Furthermore, his arm was killing him though he'd pretended otherwise with Sydney. Flesh wound or not, he'd have to be dead to ignore the steady throb that was keeping him on edge.

Leaning back in his chair, Brickman eyed first his, then Sydney's rumpled, filthy clothes. "You were supposed to be home before dark."

"I'm here now," she said. "Benno told you I wasn't trying to skip town. Someone had to do your job, to look for the man you refused to believe existed."

Brickman scowled at the barely veiled affront. "And did you find him?"

Benno squeezed Sydney's hand, signaling her to let him handle the obnoxious policeman. "We tracked the man to The Sea Breeze Apartments in Seaside. Did you run a trace on the car?"

Brickman leaned toward his desk but was obviously in no hurry to appease them. He fiddled with a manila folder, opened it and took his time checking his notes.

"The plates are registered to one William Emerson of Cannon Beach," he finally said. "The Oldsmobile, however, belongs to Henry Pollack of Seaside. He reported the car stolen three weeks ago. Emerson never even noticed the switch."

"Benno, you were right about the theft." Sydney didn't sound too surprised.

"What is the name of this mystery man?" Brickman asked her, his expression passive. "And why did you decide to look for him in Seaside?"

"His name is Al Fox. We traced him to Seaside through a liquor store receipt and an arcade token."

The noise Brickman made sounded more like a bark than a laugh. Shaking his head, he said, "Quite the amateur detectives, aren't we? Maybe I should arrest the two of you for concealing evidence."

Sydney pulled free of Benno's restraint and placed both hands on his desk. She leaned close and stared Brickman directly in the eyes. "Evidence you weren't willing to look for in the first place?"

The policeman ignored that and stared back. "So where is this Al Fox now?"

"He could be in Stone Beach for all we know," Benno said. "Someone followed us from Seaside. Took a couple of shots at us down on the beach last night."

"On the beach, huh?" He seemed to notice Benno's bloody sleeve for the first time. "He got you in all that fog? Must have been a damn good shot."

"Or a lucky one. So, how about it, Brickman?" Benno asked as Sydney straightened and offered him her silent support. "Are you ready to give a little here? We got you a name and a place to start. Two places. In addition to Seaside, you might check out the L.A. area for some history on Fox."

"Why L.A.?"

"Show him the clipping, Sydney."

When she dug into the bag that held so many items, Benno noticed she carefully removed the article from the zippered compartment. And, just as carefully, she concealed Martha's note and mother-of-pearl pen.

"We found this in his apartment." Sydney handed over the yellowed newsprint. "This proves he set me up."

Brickman's eyebrows shot up. "A vendetta?"

"Why else would he have hung on to this for three years?"

"What about a motive?"

"I can't explain it. I swear I never saw Fox before we met in Lincoln City."

Brickman added the clipping to his file. "Give me some time to work on this." His expression changing subtly, he asked, "You two won't be leaving town again today, will you?"

Not about to commit himself, Benno shrugged. "Nothing planned."

Brickman turned to Sydney. "And where will I be able to find you?"

Before she could answer, Benno ushered her toward the door. "We'll let you know."

"If I hear anything, I'll be in touch," Brickman called after them. "I expect you to do the same, not that I'm giving you license to do any investigating. But just in case you do learn something of value—no more holding out on us or I may have to reserve a jail cell for each of you."

"Don't worry, Officer Brickman," Sydney said tightly. "I wouldn't think of concealing information from you."

No sooner had they gone through the outer office and reached the sidewalk than Benno jumped on that lie.

"You wouldn't think of concealing anything?" he repeated in a low voice. "What the hell do you call hiding Martha's note and pen?"

Sydney stopped cold. "Insurance. I'm not convinced Brickman isn't involved. Martha may have plotted the murder, but she's got that man tied around her little finger."

"According to Kenneth, Brickman started sniffing at Martha's heels the moment he saw her, but she's never given him a second look."

"Until now. How do we know Brickman's not involved?" Sydney demanded. "Don't you think it's curious that he accepted what we had to tell him so easily? He's never believed me before."

A passerby knocked into Benno's wounded arm. He flinched and cursed under his breath.

"Maybe it's the wound," he said with a groan. "Maybe that convinced him we're on to something."

"And maybe he already knew about it. How did the assailant know how to find us?"

"Assuming it was Fox—from Vita."

"Or from Officer Mick Brickman. You did tell him we were going to Seaside," Sydney reminded him. "Who's to say it wasn't Brickman himself waiting for us. He does have a gun."

"Too bad I didn't take the bullet. If I had, we could have dug it out to see if it matched the ones fired from Brickman's gun."

Sydney's jaw tightened. "Go ahead, joke all you want. I say Brickman needs watching."

"Brickman is ineffectual."

But underneath, Benno suspected she could be correct.

When the bullet had grazed him, he'd wondered for a second which of them had been the intended target—despite what the clipping implied. Thoughts of a vendetta being played out against him kept crossing his mind. Brickman had always cozied up to Parnell Anderson....

Too much to take in until he could think straight, Benno decided, cradling his arm.

And Sydney was staring at him doing so. "Are you ready to see a doctor yet?"

"I don't need a doctor," he hedged. Surely an antiseptic would prevent infection and a few painkillers would put him out of his misery for a while.

"You'll see a doctor anyway, if I have anything to say about it."

He didn't savor her determined expression. She was going to be a pain in the butt until he gave way. He might as well make the most of the situation.

"All right, I'll cut you a deal. I'll go to a doctor if you agree not to stay at a motel."

Sydney frowned. "Martha isn't going to let me live temporarily at her brother's house."

"But you can stay at mine."

The frown deepened. "I don't know...."

"Do you really want to be alone in light of everything that has been happening? You could be a sitting duck, an easy target for a murderer."

Benno could tell that idea didn't thrill Sydney. Before she could refuse his offer, he headed for the Thunderbird that was parked several yards away. Luckily, a couple of healthy teenagers had helped him free the car from the sand when he and Sydney had left their hiding place that morning.

Opening the driver's door, he insisted, "You'll be safer at my place."

"I'm not so sure about that," she muttered, going around to the passenger side.

Benno clenched his jaw. Sensing Sydney's confusion about him had kept him awake most of the night. Too much time to think. Too many bad memories, especially surrounding The Sugar Loaf, which seemed destined to forever play an important role in his life. He threw himself into the driver's seat and started the engine. He wondered if the things he'd told Sydney about his background had had a chance to sink in and turn her off. And if those confessions had disturbed her, what would she think if she knew what had happened that fateful night twenty years ago?

Whatever the reason, he was feeling like hell and not liking it one bit.

"Let's stop playing games here." His temper flaring as he faced her, he made it an order rather than a request. "What we're involved in is serious business.

You're going to move in with me for your own good. I won't touch you, if that's what you're worried about.''

Sydney immediately softened. "Benno, no. Don't think such a thing.''

Coolly, he said, "Good.'' He concentrated on pulling the car out of the parking spot. Best that he keep his emotional distance. "Then you have no reason to refuse.''

"But first we're going to get you to a doctor," she said, her tone resigned.

Benno was feeling anything but resigned. He was filthy and hungry and bad-tempered. He never should have complicated his life with a stranger's problems. A loner by conditioning, he should have stuck to his code and stayed uninvolved.

Then maybe he wouldn't be hurting, either outside or in.

THROUGH THE SLITS OF Venetian blinds, he watched the Thunderbird pull away.

Game time was over.

He was frustrated and yet bored, tired of playing cat and mouse. He'd almost blown it the night before. He couldn't take any more chances or he might lose everything.

The Raferty woman wasn't going to break on her own, so he would have to get rid of her in the most expedient way and make it *look* like suicide.

He would do it tonight.

Chapter Eleven

Benno's cottage was the building nearest the beach on a cul-de-sac west of Main Street. It reminded Sydney of the man himself. Having weathered countless storms, the small house remained proud, unbroken, solitary.

Standing over his bed, she listened to Benno's deep, slow breathing. He'd passed out, the combination of exhaustion and painkillers prescribed by the doctor too much for him to fight.

Golden light streamed through a break in the curtains, darting a shaft across the bed. The white gauze protecting Benno's wounded arm gleamed against his olive skin. His chest was bare but for a silky matting of hair. The knowledge that he might be naked beneath the sheets stirred her.

Thick stubble shadowed his face, making his chin scar more prominent. He was as tough as they came. And yet, asleep, Benno projected an innocent quality, the very idea at odds with Sydney's image of the dark knight who rushed headlong into danger.

She moved away from the bed and adjusted the window coverings. A cool darkness pervaded the room as she edged out quietly and closed the door. A cozy one-story, Benno's cottage consisted of a living room, kitchen, two small bedrooms and a single bath. She'd been thrilled to move in temporarily, if for no other reason than to bid Martha Lord good riddance.

Shaking away the unpleasant memory of their unfond farewell, she picked up the telephone and punched out a Seattle number she had looked up in her address book.

While she waited for someone to answer, she looked around with pleasure and a sense of peace. The decor reflected the view out the windows. Sand-colored walls. Love seat and couch in a muted wildgrass print. A coffee table with a driftwood base, glass top decorated with shells and a single starfish.

Three rings and a connection was made.

"This is Honor," came a low, husky, prerecorded voice. "Sorry that Nora and I are busy, but if you leave your name and number, I'll get back to you as soon as possible."

Sydney decided to hang up rather than leave some obscure warning that might frighten Honor, when undoubtedly the actress wasn't even involved in this mess.

Arms folded tightly across her chest, she approached the fireplace and studied the canvas hanging above the mantel—The Sugar Loaf, painted not on a sunny day, but on a stormy one. The sky was dark and threatening, the sea roiling and careening up the seastack's rocky sides. Recognizing the danger they'd been in more clearly than before, she rubbed her arms and turned away from the oil painting.

The bay windows on the opposite wall gave her a perfect vista of the beach to the north. With a start, she realized Benno had a clear if distant view of the unusually shaped seastack that had played such an important part first in his life, now in hers.

Too restless to sit and wait for him to awaken, she decided to take a stroll along the beach. Quietly, she left the cottage. The sun shone brightly over the sand as if the storm had never occurred. She glanced back at Benno's house with its peeling white paint and sea-blue outside shutters that would keep the winter storms at bay. Then she turned north and was drawn inexorably to The Sugar Loaf.

A comfortable pace brought her to the boulder-strewn area in less than ten minutes. A few children played in the shallows and a teenager sat on a shelf halfway up the north side. No one paid any attention to her as they scrambled over rocky ledges pocked with cracks.

At the base of the seastack, several depressions formed perfect tidal pools partly filled with seawater where lush carpets of brown and green seaweed protected clusters of barnacles and blue mussels. She spotted a purple starfish and several colorful sea urchins with three-inch spines. Green sea anemones shimmered on the tidal pool's floor.

So much life had almost been the host to death twelve hours earlier.

Almost.

If Benno had died trying to save her, she would have been burdened with guilt for the rest of her days. If she had come away alive without him to guide her to safety...

But they were both alive, and she had come away with something very different than guilt, a knowledge at once exhilarating and unwelcome.

Nestled together in the heart of cold compassion-
less rock, they had shared something warm and
special. Something alarming. Sydney had to face the
fact that her feelings for Benno had gone beyond mere
caring. No matter how much she rationalized, no
matter how many times she reminded herself that
she'd believed herself in love with an impostor barely
a week before, she couldn't shake the fact: She was in
love with Benno DeMartino.

Now what was she going to do about it?

Discomfort and indecision sweeping through her,
Sydney decided to get away from The Sugar Loaf and
head back toward the cottage via Main Street. Since
Benno wouldn't be awake for a while, she might as
well browse through the shops. Hotfooting it over the
sand strip and along another cul-de-sac, she headed
toward the center of town.

Her enthusiasm was short-lived. Though she studied the merchandise displayed in the store windows,
she didn't bother to go into any of the shops. Her
thoughts kept wandering to Benno.

Had he awakened?

Would he be anxious when he didn't find her there?

About to give up the pretense of shopping altogether, Sydney was alerted when she drew near Stone
Beach Photos.

Standing on the curb several yards away, Parnell
Anderson and Mick Brickman were huddled to-
gether. Their conversation seemed almost conspira-
torial and she was reminded of the memorial service.
Of the two men, Parnell seemed the more forceful.
The leader. Whatever he was saying was putting
Brickman out of sorts. The policeman's fists were
wedged at his hips and his face was drawn into a scowl.

Sydney couldn't help herself. Feigning interest in a window display she didn't really care about, she edged her way closer and did her best to eavesdrop while watching the men's reflections in the glass.

"This is the best opportunity we've had to nail him," Parnell was saying, "so don't blow it."

Brickman opened his mouth to answer, then noticed Sydney's presence. Their eyes met in the window. His jaw snapped shut and he inclined his head to his companion. Parnell turned and caught sight of her. When he motioned the other man away, Brickman left immediately.

Disappointed that she hadn't heard more, Sydney started to move along herself but was brought up short when Parnell Anderson suddenly stopped her.

"Miss Raferty," he said, standing directly in her path. "I hear you've been having yourself some trouble."

"Not of my own making."

"No, not unless you count the company you keep."

Figuring he meant Benno, whom he didn't like, she merely said, "Really?"

"I heard you moved in with DeMartino."

"He was kind enough to lend me his guest bedroom—not that it's any of your business."

"You don't have to justify your sleeping arrangements as long as you're satisfied."

Outraged, Sydney tried to brush past him, but Parnell used his arm as a barricade.

"What is it you want?" she asked through gritted teeth.

"To warn you about DeMartino."

"I don't need your warnings."

"I think you do." He lowered his arm and sounded like a cat that had cornered a tasty snack when he said, "I would lay odds that he never told you why he left town only two days before high school graduation."

"Maybe he did tell me."

Parnell took a close look at her expression. His lips drew into a smirk. "I didn't think so."

"When and if Benno wants to tell me," Sydney said, showing an indifference she wasn't feeling, "I'll be happy to listen."

"I doubt that he'd tell you the truth."

"Which is?"

Parnell's nasty smile faded. "That he killed my kid sister."

"You're lying!"

"Ask anyone in town, Miss Raferty. Ask *him* what happened to Nissa. If he won't tell you, come back to see me and I will. My office is just up the street," he said, pointing to a small complex. "I'm listed on the directory."

With that, he inclined his head and departed.

And Sydney stood staring after him, her insides cold with dread, her heartbeat accelerating until she felt ready to burst.

Could it be true?

Could Benno really have taken a life?

It would explain so much. Another reason why he was so secretive. Why he'd been gone from Stone Beach for so many years. Why he was still disliked. The dreadful incident in his past the Tarot had implied.

If it was true. Her every instinct wanted to deny the possibility.

Feeling like Alice who'd stepped through the looking glass, Sydney ran along Main Street, not planning to stop until she arrived at Benno's cottage. She had to find out whether or not she could have been so fooled by yet another man!

If she had... if she were wrong about Benno...

Where the hell were her psychic gifts when she really needed them? Sydney wondered yet again. Why couldn't she look within herself and see the truth?

As the cottage came within sight, Sydney realized she'd never been so frightened in her life.

BENNO AWOKE WITH A START. The room was dark. It took him a minute to reorient himself. He was in his own bed. The curtains were closed. Gingerly, he moved his arm. Tender, but the throbbing had stopped. Sydney had been right to bully him into seeing a doctor.

Sydney.

He had an immediate urge to see her.

Rolling out of bed, he removed his jeans from a nearby clothes tree and stepped into them. He was pulling up the zipper when he opened the door and walked barefoot into the living room.

"Sydney?"

The house was quiet, eerily so. Benno strode to the other bedroom and banged open the door. No Sydney.

"Damn!"

Where could she have gone. He was on his way to his bedroom to grab a shirt and shoes so he could go looking for her when he glanced out the bay window. Expelling a sigh of relief, he allowed his tense muscles to sag when he spotted her.

Even though she looked as angry as a wet hen, Benno hadn't ever seen a more welcome sight.

She was safe.

He opened the door and waited on the stoop. When she came within hearing distance, he asked, "Who got your dander up?"

Instead of answering, she gave him a searching look as she passed him. Worried, he followed her back into the house. About to try a different approach, he stopped when he realized she was working herself up to say something. Her cheeks were flushed, her forehead creased, her eyes wide with a stricken look that scared the hell out of him.

"Tell me about Nissa."

The breath caught in his throat and his chest squeezed tight. "Who have you been talking to?"

She didn't answer, merely leaned back against the love seat, crossed her arms over her chest and waited.

He should have known she would find out sooner or later, Benno thought. He should have told her himself. Now she would probably despise him.

"Nissa was...a friend...one of the few I had in this town. Like Kenneth, she came from the right side of the tracks. Nissa had everything—brains, beauty, class—and Parnell Anderson for a brother. But you already know that, right?" Would she hate him now? he wondered. "What did he tell you, Sydney?"

"That you killed his sister." She paused for a beat, then asked, "Well, aren't you going to deny it?"

"No." The guilt that had plagued him all these years was never far away. "It was my fault," he admitted, remembering.

He stopped at the window and looked out.

"What happened?" Sydney asked, sounding controlled.

"We were holed up in The Sugar Loaf—Kenneth, Nissa and me. It was a crummy night, raining off and on." He could feel the damp settle in his bones as if it were yesterday. He would never forget the feeling. Never. "I'd gotten my hands on a six-pack and we lost track of time drinking and making jokes about graduating in a couple of weeks."

"Parnell said you left town two days before graduation," Sydney interrupted.

Caught up by the past, Benno barely noticed she'd spoken. "It was a stupid fight about the prom. Nissa expected me to take her, but I was busted. Pa had wandered off somewhere the week before. I worked, but I had to eat, you know? Anyway, Nissa didn't care that I didn't have the money. Said she had enough to pay for everything. Me and my dumb pride!"

He began pacing as if the simple activity could release him from the wired feeling he was experiencing.

"I couldn't just say no and thank her for being so sweet. When she insisted, I got angry and told her what she could do with her money. I called her a spoiled little rich girl."

"One who obviously cared about you."

As he had cared about her, Benno thought, cursing himself for the millionth time that the last words he'd spoken to Nissa had been harsh. He swept a hand over his eyes but couldn't wipe away the memory.

"She started to cry. I'll never forget the look on her face before she ran out of the cave. I tried to tell myself that she'd be better off without me. If Kenneth hadn't called me a jerk and suggested I go after her, I might never have known what really happened to Nissa.''

"The tide," Sydney murmured, her tautness receding.

"I couldn't stop her," Benno said, not any more than he was able to stop himself from reliving the painful memory. His chest was so tight he could hardly breathe. "She was already making her way down. It shouldn't have happened!" he cried. "Nissa was surefooted, used to the climb. But I'd given her that beer and she was being a little reckless. If I'd gone after her thirty seconds sooner..."

Benno took a deep breath and closed his eyes. He could see Nissa's terrified expression as if the tragedy was happening now, before his very eyes. That expression had haunted him all these years. It was as if a photograph had been permanently implanted in his brain.

"She lost her balance and a breaker washed her right off the face of the rock."

"Oh, my God. That must have been awful."

"The current sucked her under—" his voice broke and he took a deep breath "—just like that." His heartbeat had accelerated and his pulse was pounding as it had been that night. "I tried to go after her, but Kenneth held me back, told me not to be stupid...no reason for me to chance drowning before we even spotted her. He flashed a light all around but all we saw were swells of water. No Nissa. Not even a trace."

"You loved her, didn't you?" Sydney asked.

"Up until recently, Nissa was the best thing that ever happened to me," Benno said.

And now Sydney was. But how could he tell her? The daughter of a judge, she was out of his class, too.

He was no better for her than he'd been for Nissa. Knowing didn't stop him from wanting. That had always been his problem.

"I was no good for Nissa," he said, "and I should have known that I would be responsible for ruining her life, if not for taking it away altogether."

Sydney noticed his voice had grown softer as he spoke. The back of her eyelids stung. Such a senseless loss, but certainly not what Parnell had wanted her to believe.

"Nissa's death was an accident, Benno, no matter what her brother says. And you had no way of knowing something so awful would happen when she left the cave."

Sydney remembered asking Benno what the dumbest thing he'd ever done was and he'd responded that it had been getting involved with the wrong person. She'd completely misinterpreted his statement at the time, but now she understood. He felt that if he hadn't been involved with Nissa, she would still be alive. With a sense of relief, and with a measure of guilt for doubting Benno, she reached out to him.

"You can't blame yourself forever," she said, touching his bare shoulder. His flesh was warm and vibrant beneath her fingers.

"You don't forget something like that, Sydney." Benno's eyes were haunted, but he covered her hand with his. "The memory stays with you, even when you do your best to forget."

"Maybe if you hadn't left town..."

"They would never have let me live down Nissa's death," he insisted, pulling away from Sydney. He moved to the fireplace and stared at the painting. "A nothing like me lives while one of the respectable ones dies?"

How sad that he should have such a low opinion of himself. "And so you went in search of respectability."

"Not at first. I just left because I couldn't stay, not after seeing her body when it washed up. Not after the accusations." He turned to face her and leaned against the mantelpiece. "The mighty Andersons wanted me to pay for Nissa's death. Old Man Anderson kicked my butt up one side and down the other. And I let him. If Kenneth hadn't been with Nissa and me at The Sugar Loaf that night, I would have landed in the slammer. At the time, I thought I deserved to be in jail."

Realizing that Benno was being more open than he'd ever been with her, Sydney pressed on. "What about your father?"

"What about him?"

"Didn't he support you?"

Benno laughed. "Pa came home for a week, commiserated when I got beat up, then drank himself into a stupor. I hated my life, and with Nissa gone, there wasn't any reason to stay in Stone Beach."

"Where did you go? How did you survive?"

"Any way I could. I did any menial job I could get, worked my way down the northwest coast, always trying to forget my guilt, never quite succeeding. I did have success running a coffeehouse-bar in a southern California town these past few years, however."

"Obviously that wasn't enough."

"You're right. All the while I knew someday I'd have to prove I wasn't a worthless no-good bum like Pa. No one knows what happened to him. One day he wandered off and never came back. I used to tell myself he was looking for my mother when he went off on his excursions.''

"Maybe he found her.''

Benno shrugged. "Maybe. A couple of months ago I came back to Stone Beach and opened a second business. In spite of Parnell Anderson's efforts to force me out, Benno's Place is doing okay. Some of the locals don't know Anderson, and the tourists wouldn't care if they did.'' He moved away from the fireplace. "When you came to town, I was back in California, making legal arrangements to give my manager a cut of my place there as an incentive to keep the profits healthy. I'm not planning to go back there in the near future.''

Things began to click into place, especially the reference to justice Parnell made in the photo shop.

"Parnell has held you and Kenneth responsible for Nissa's death all these years, hasn't he?'' Sydney asked, her growing realization spurring a renewed anger. "So he had a motive for wanting Kenneth dead. But you didn't tell me. All this time, you let me think you were helping me out of the goodness of your heart!''

Benno had the grace to look contrite, and yet he touched her cheek and said, "I was trying to protect you because I was afraid it was my fault that you'd been dragged into the mess.''

An excuse! Sydney slapped his hand away. "But you didn't tell me that. You had a hidden agenda all along,'' she accused, quickly working herself into a rage. "You're no different than Al Fox!''

"I *am* different,'' Benno insisted, stepping closer. He almost sounded desperate that she believe him when he said, "I love you. I've never felt this way about a woman before!"

"Pardon me if I have trouble believing that."

"If you don't, it's because you don't want to. You felt the same way I did in The Sugar Loaf last night. You wanted to make love to me. But you withdrew and now I know why. The things I told you about my past were too much for you to handle. I can imagine what you think of me now."

Sydney sensed Benno's very real hurt. But could she trust her own intuition? She vacillated. Her insight hadn't been the most reliable lately, true, but could she really go through life questioning every person she met, everything she felt?

"I don't think any less of you because of Nissa," she said, regaining her calm. "You're harder on yourself than anyone could be...other than her brother. But I prize honesty, Benno, especially after what Fox put me through."

"Then I promise I'll be as honest as I know how."

"I'm not sure that's good enough."

"My word is all I have to offer."

They stared at each other. Her move. Sydney knew Benno wouldn't push himself on her. If she believed that, why couldn't she trust him completely?

"I want to believe you," she told him.

Sydney remembered when he'd said the same to her. Everyone else had thought she was crazy, but not Benno.

"That's a start."

A start was enough to propel Benno into action. He took her in his arms as he'd done so often during the past week. But this time he wasn't trying to comfort or reassure her, Sydney thought. And this time, her awareness of him reached new heights. His stubble scraped her forehead, a small hurt that made her feel alive. His solid flesh against hers sent a flame coursing through her veins more powerful than her now fading anger. The silky matting on his chest burned her palm.

"I would never do anything to deliberately hurt you," Benno murmured. "But perhaps you think it best if we didn't explore any further what we could have together. I'm not a safe person to be around."

"The dark knight rushing headlong into danger," she whispered.

"What?"

"Nothing," she murmured. "Just a fantasy."

He cradled her head, stared into her eyes, undoubtedly waiting for a signal that she believed, trusted and wanted him. Pulse ragged, Sydney wondered if she was being a fool. If only the insights she had about her own life were as accurate as those she had about other people's. She'd known Lex had meant trouble for her friend Candace without ever having met the man, but she hadn't been able to see the truth about Kenneth face-to-face.

Consequently, Sydney wondered if she could trust her own judgment.

She loved him, Sydney reminded herself. What he'd been hiding from her was his own profound hurt. Nissa had been the best thing that had happened to him until recently, he'd said. Until recently, when he'd fallen for her?

"I do love you," he whispered as if he were the one with psychic abilities.

The time for indecision over, she tangled her fingers in his loose hair and drew his head down as she raised her face. Their lips touched, sweetly at first, then more passionately as she loosened her reserve.

Without freeing her mouth, Benno lifted her. Sydney made a futile attempt to protest and make him release her. Afraid she might hurt his wounded arm, she clung to his neck and readjusted her weight. As easily as if she were a feather, he carried her into the bedroom. Setting her down on the bed, he removed her khaki trousers and lace-trimmed briefs. She gasped as his fingers trailed down her thighs, calves, ankles, before freeing her completely of the garments.

Dressed only in an oversize coral T-shirt and a pair of dangly shell earrings, Sydney curled her legs under her and reached out to unzip Benno's jeans. No underwear. Even in the darkened room she could see he was ready for her. She touched him intimately. His jeans had barely hit the floor when Benno lunged and in one smooth motion had her pinned under him lengthwise.

Sydney had trouble breathing as she looked up into Benno's eyes—not that he was crushing her with his weight. Fear stalked her even as she was about to capitulate. As if he sensed her insecurity, he waited. Their ragged breaths filled the quiet room with the sound of delayed consummation. Sydney touched his face, slid her hand under his fall of satin-dark hair, ran a finger around the diamond stud in his ear, yet never gave him leave to look away.

She held him captive as she attempted to look into his soul and hoped that this once she would receive a true message.

What she saw reflected through his eyes was love. She sensed a rightness to this union she hadn't felt with her supposed husband. While she'd been happy at the time—relieved to find a positive force in her life—she hadn't experienced the joy she did at this moment.

"I love you, Benno," she admitted, spontaneously and without reservation.

"I know."

Benno slid the oversize T-shirt up over her hips. Without breaking eye contact, he smoothed a hand over her belly and between her thighs to prepare her for him. With a sigh, Sydney lowered her lids. Responding sinuously, she arched her body and felt relief when he finally entered her. This joining was right and true, she thought, unlike the last time.

But even as she gave herself up to a desire that seemed to rage through her, Sydney was saddened. In a short time, she hoped, the real murderer would be apprehended and she would be safe. And soon after that, Stone Beach would be no more than a memory.

The thought brought tears to her eyes and an intense finale to their lovemaking. When Benno lay over her, whispering her name and words of love, she felt her own betrayal beginning.

For, rather than responding, rather than concentrating on him and the love they shared, Sydney thought of motives and suspects. Revenge rather than greed. Parnell Anderson instead of Martha Lord.

Fear could be more powerful than love, she realized. Fear made her want to protect herself from another hurt even now. Benno rolled off her and onto his back. He stared up at the ceiling in silence.

He knew, Sydney realized, and yet he said nothing.

She was certain Benno knew that, once her name was cleared, she intended to leave him as had every person he had ever loved.

Chapter Twelve

"Well, look who the cat dragged in," Poppy said as Sydney followed Benno inside his establishment several hours later. Almost finished removing chairs from the tables, the barmaid set one upright with a bang. "I thought I was going to have the pleasure of running this place all by myself on a Saturday night, too. I can't tell you how much fun last night was. You're lucky I didn't walk out and leave this place up for grabs."

"Didn't anyone ever tell you you're not supposed to give a man who's been shot a hard time?" Benno asked.

"I heard it was only a flesh wound."

"And I was hoping you'd be worried."

Sydney remained silent through their bickering. At least Benno had loosened up and was talking freely with his employee, if not with her.

He'd been introspective since their lovemaking, and she hadn't had the words or the will to open him up. Avoidance of a difficult subject seemed the safest route. She would have stayed at the cottage to keep her distance if Benno hadn't insisted she come with him for her own protection, though, truthfully, she hadn't really wanted to be alone.

"So, is the boss putting you to work tonight?" Poppy asked as Sydney propped herself on a stool at the bar.

"I wouldn't mind."

"Maybe you could read your cards for the customers," Benno said sarcastically. "Give them some great insights into their character. Tell them what terrific futures *they're* going to have."

Sydney flushed and avoided his eyes.

"Tarot?" Poppy asked enthusiastically, her irritation with her employer fading. "You really know how to tell fortunes?" she asked Sydney who responded with a shrug. "That's a great idea! Benno, you're a genius."

"I was kidding."

"I'm not. This place is kind of a throwback to the late sixties, early seventies, more like a coffeehouse than real bar. Tarot card readings would fit right in and bring more customers. Come on," the barmaid urged. "What do you say? Let's try it."

"It's up to Sydney... like everything else."

Tension rife between them, they stared at each other.

Poppy eyed them both. "Uh-oh, maybe I shoulda kept my mouth shut, huh?"

"No," Sydney said, turning her attention to the other woman. "I'd love to read the Tarot—it would be fun." And would keep her mind off Benno and the dilemma he presented. Because he was frowning at her, she added for his benefit, "But if you don't want me to play fortune teller, Benno, say so."

"I wouldn't think of telling you what to do," he said coolly. "I learned a long time ago not to have any expectations. That way, you can't be disappointed."

But he did have expectations of her that had nothing to do with the Tarot, Sydney knew. And she'd already disappointed him. The invisible barrier between them didn't make her happy, though she'd been responsible for creating it.

Weakening in her resolve, she tried to assuage his feelings. "Want me to read your cards again?"

"Not on your life, lady. You know too much about me as it is." He turned away and signaled to Poppy. "Since you're so hot on it, go get your fortune told."

Telling herself she'd deserved the rejection, Sydney made herself comfortable at a table for two in a corner near the door. She slipped the pouch holding the tarot cards from the pocket of her long, denim skirt. All the while she laid out the spread and began her reading, she was aware of Benno's eyes on her. She tried to shake the guilt from her shoulders and concentrate, but it was difficult to do. At least Poppy made an enthusiastic questioner, even if the barmaid didn't hear what she was hoping for.

"So you can't tell me who my next husband will be, huh?" she asked.

Sydney grinned at the other woman's exaggerated expression of disappointment. "I'm afraid the cards aren't that specific."

"Shoot. I was hoping to get some guidance this time. My record with men—especially with husbands—stinks."

Several locals entered and took a large round table in the middle of the room. A family of tourists drifted in directly behind them.

"Whoops. Gotta go or the boss'll get mad."

The barmaid left to take their orders, at the same time informing the customers of the new entertainment—Sydney. Within minutes, she was busy reading another spread, and as the night progressed she had a steady stream of interested takers who wanted insights into their futures.

Giving them what they wanted kept her busy and amused and her mind off her problems.

But, at the same time, she couldn't shake her awareness of the man she loved as he went about his business. He seemed so comfortable chatting with the customers, especially the tourists. He probably put them at ease as he had her that first night she met him. Despite Poppy's comment that they needed something to boost business, the room was jammed with people.

Between readings, Sydney stared at Benno and with longing memorized every detail about him. His skin-tight jeans and midnight-blue shirt with silver buttons fastened to the neck. His dark hair tied back with a silver cord. His wrist wrapped with an elaborately tooled silver eagle. Benno was the very essence of masculinity, a pleasure she had experienced firsthand.

So why wasn't she basking in the afterglow instead of trying to make a break? When he glanced her way, his expression held the same question.

She came up with an answer: fear made people do stupid things.

He looked straight at her, making Sydney's cheeks grow warm. A lump formed in her throat and she concentrated on the cards in her hand. What would they tell her, she wondered, if she asked them about her relationship with Benno? Would they advise her to trust him and stay or to run from another entanglement as fast as she could?

Maybe she was wrong to let her own fears of repeating a mistake keep her from realizing her own happiness.

She shuffled the deck and cut the cards using the hand closest to her heart. All night she'd been reading the Tarot for fun, but this time, she sought real insight, an answer to what might be the hardest decision she'd ever have to make.

Sydney focused inward, freeing herself of her usual constraints, willing herself to see the truth. She began the spread and tried to remain objective until she'd turned the last card.

But the Ten of Swords—all of which were implanted in a man's back—confirmed the unfavorable and highly serious implications of this reading heralded by four cards of the Major Arcana.

Her significator, the Hermit reversed, indicated her overdependence on others. The Chariot reflected the great ordeal she was going through. Temperance in her recent past showed her to be straddling the middle road, and Magician as self indicated that she had the power to make things happen.

But what?

The positions of two cards next to each other made her most uncomfortable. The figure in the Five of Cups had its back turned to the Knight of Swords— Benno's card. The three spilled cups could indicate loss and bereavement, her turning her back on Benno and leaving him. Then, again, the two upright cups might symbolize a union that couldn't be destroyed.

Which way to interpret these two cards?

Sydney sensed her decision to accept the loss or to hold on to him would directly affect Benno. The Ten of Swords implied she had the power to destroy him.

Stricken, Sydney stared at the spread. Concentrated her energy. If ever she needed help above what common sense and natural intuition could give her, now was the time. She blocked out the sights and sounds and smells of the room and looked into her own heart and soul. She had to go deeper to know how to decode the cards' message.

A mistake could prove fatal to the man she loved.

At the thought, a chill crawled through her limbs and enveloped her heart. Her sense of the present receded, first slowly, then more rapidly. She became disoriented as she entered a blackness deeper than any she'd experienced.

Trapped by the dark.

Suffocating.

Inside her mind, she struggled to find her way to safety. No exit. Danger everywhere.

Terrified, she grew frenzied. Her lungs on the verge of collapse, she burst free of her inner prison.

Benno was running toward her as if in slow motion. His mouth was moving, his lips forming her name. His arms were stretched out, reaching for her. Trying to protect her, Sydney realized. A mysterious figure blocked her view of the man she loved. The presence brought Benno's approach to an abrupt halt. She felt his pain as he sprawled to the ground and was unable to rise.

Then she saw the gun, the same one she'd seen in her dream. With painstaking slowness, the barrel revolved toward the spot where Benno lay....

"No!"

Her eyes flew open and Sydney took a quick look around to see if anyone had heard. No one seemed at all perturbed.

Though she was once more in the present, her sense of unreality swayed with her. People were talking, but their words sounded garbled, meant nothing to her confused mind. She was disoriented and a little shaky, and a light coating of perspiration covered her entire body.

Reluctantly, she returned her attention to the spread.

Heart racing, Sydney saw the truth. She needed to stop being overly dependent and to stop taking the middle road about their relationship. In order to save Benno, she must turn her back on him as the figure in the cups card did to the dark knight. She had to start acting alone to clear her name before it was too late. If she hesitated now, Benno would be the one to suffer. Her premonitions might be sightly askew, but they always held some basic truth.

Hands trembling, she gathered the cards together and slipped them into their pouch.

But what to do?

Her gaze traveled around the crowded room, coming to rest on two newcomers who were claiming the last vacant table. Mick Brickman and Martha Lord. The man was being conciliatory, wrapping a black leather jacket around the young woman's bare shoulders.

Why would either of them come into Benno's Place unless it was to make trouble? Sydney wondered.

The two were acting awfully familiar, but she couldn't fathom Martha's being interested in Brickman unless she was using him. And, despite the fact that Parnell Anderson had a motive for killing Kenneth, Sydney didn't believe he had anything to do with the murder, not after finding Martha's mechanical pencil in the car Al Fox had stolen. Thank God she hadn't turned it and the note over to Brickman.

Rather than dwelling on her suspicions, Sydney realized the opportunity the couple's presence gave her. Benno was busy filling orders at the bar, his attention definitely caught by his work.

She rose, and, slipping her cards into the pocket of her long denim skirt, quietly left. She would take the opportunity to finish the search she and Benno had begun.

If she was lucky, she would somehow find out the murderer's identity in the house on the cliff.

AFTER CATCHING UP with a backlog of orders, Benno looked around the room and caught sight of Martha and Brickman at a table for two. He couldn't resist approaching to give them a hard time.

"I didn't know you two were an item."

"You have a problem with that?" Brickman asked.

Benno looked directly at Martha who wasn't dressed with her usual panache—the biker's jacket was in dramatic contrast to her strapless dress.

"No problem," he answered. "Not as long as it doesn't interfere with your work—and judgment."

Martha's face grew red and pinched looking. "How dare you imply—"

"I'm not implying anything. I'm saying I don't believe you'd attach yourself to a man of little means." He gave the policeman a searching look. "No offense, Brickman, but you have to admit your date has a prime motive for murder, and therefore a motive for cozying up with the law."

"That's enough, DeMartino!" Brickman growled.

Benno backed off. "I can take a hint. You two enjoy your evening now."

"Brick, I told you this was a bad idea," Martha said in a low tone. "I want out of here."

Benno eyed Sydney's corner table and was surprised to see it occupied by a couple of locals. He'd glanced her way often enough while working, but hadn't noticed she was gone until now. His gaze skimmed the rest of the room. No Sydney. She wasn't at the bar talking to Poppy, either. His barmaid was alone, flipping a couple of burgers on the grill.

Approaching Poppy, he asked, "Have you seen Sydney?"

"She's not here."

Worry made him snap, "And you just let her leave?"

Poppy seemed startled. "I didn't know I was supposed to be her jailer."

"Where did she go?"

"How am I supposed to know? She left right after Martha Lord waltzed in here with Brick. Boy, I wonder what he wants with a tramp like her." She flashed the couple in question a resentful look. "Stupid question," she muttered.

Not about to get involved in a conversation about Poppy's ex-husband, Benno said, "Hold down the fort for a while, would you? I have to go after Sydney before she gets herself into trouble."

"Oh, no, you're not leaving me to run this place by myself *again*."

"You're terrific," he assured her, already on his way. "We'll talk raise tomorrow."

"A *major* raise," Poppy added loudly.

As he dashed to the door, Benno almost ran into Martha.

"Watch where you're going!" she said, jumping back.

Benno circled her and kept going. Before exiting, he glanced over his shoulder and realized Martha was staring after him. And Brickman was nowhere in sight. Had she been listening to his conversation with Poppy? Even if she had, Martha couldn't possibly know where he thought Sydney had gone.

He raced down to the corner where he'd left his Thunderbird. The full moon was bright in a cloudless sky, the rising winds the only indication the weather might turn during the night. Getting into his car, Benno hoped against hope that Sydney hadn't gone back to the Lord house.

He checked his cottage first, calling her name and checking every room. No Sydney. Kenneth's house was a safe bet. He couldn't understand why she would go there alone. Surely she recognized the potential danger.

Afraid he was already too late, he gunned the accelerator and turned the Thunderbird toward the house on the cliff.

DISAPPOINTED THAT SHE HADN'T found anything more to implicate Martha after a quick search of the other woman's bedroom, Sydney headed downstairs for Kenneth's study.

The wind rattled around the house. A loose shutter banged somewhere nearby and made Sydney jump.

She sucked in a deep breath. She couldn't help being a bit spooked. Breaking and entering was not the easiest thing in the world to do for a person who had more than once been called a "straight arrow," though technically she hadn't broken anything since she still had the front door key.

To distract herself from any untoward imaginings, Sydney concentrated on the pieces of the puzzle they'd found—something she'd been doing off and on since she'd left Benno's Place.

Something kept niggling at her, some detail she was positive she was missing. The register tape and arcade token were of no further use. But the newspaper clipping and mechanical pencil were of significance, as was the note. If only she knew whether Martha had sent the note to Al Fox or to someone else—say Mick Brickman.

Could the three of them be working together?

She entered the study and turned on the room light, wondering where Benno had left off in his search. There was no point going over the ground he'd already covered.

The large first-floor room made a comfortable yet fairly informal office for a working architect. Leather couch and chairs surrounding a fireplace. Drawing table set between two long windows. Teak storage unit with a rolltop desk hugging the wall opposite.

She decided to start her search with the file drawers that were part of the wall unit.

Kenneth Lord certainly had been organized. The hanging files with matching interior folders alternated in color—gold, red, blue, gold, red, blue—and their identification tabs were set precisely in five stairstep positions.

About to pull the first file, Sydney froze when she heard a noise outside she couldn't identify. Someone returning to the house? Though she listened intently, no other sound followed but the scraping of a tree limb on the upper story. No doubt the wind had blown some loose object against the house.

Breathing normally again, she got to work, checking file after file, skimming through the folders within, but finding nothing obvious. Only when she finished all three drawers did she think to take a more objective look inside. She started over.

When she reopened the middle drawer, something about the color coding didn't seem quite right. Gold, red, blue . . . gold, red, blue . . . gold . . .

A red file was missing from the center of the drawer! The gold file on one side of the empty spot was labeled Kramer, James, the blue file, Lundquist, Helga.

Resolved to identify that missing red file, Sydney began by checking the desk area as well as the drawers and shelves of the wall unit, all the while fighting the uneasy sensation that made her want to look over her shoulder. A frisson of fear settled in her chest and blossomed. She was being silly, she assured herself in an attempt to shake the feeling. If Martha returned, she would hear the car.

She ordered herself to concentrate in the meantime, to try to pinpoint what it was that was still nagging at her—something she'd missed in going over what she and Benno knew about the murder.

The murder.

To the best of her ability, Sydney replayed first the dream and then the reality. What did she know from either? The only clue had been a small metal stud found in Kenneth's closed fist. In the dream she'd seen him rip something from his assailant's sleeve while falling.

She thought about the stud and its possible source.

Metal studs sometimes decorated fancy shirts ... or leather jackets, and she'd seen Brickman slip a black leather jacket around Martha's shoulders that very night.

Brickman's jacket? Or Martha's? How could she find out?

She examined one of the higher shelves of the wall unit, feeling behind a speaker, part of an elaborate sound system. No missing folder. Trying not to lose heart, she thoroughly searched the drawing table and the sitting area, including the magazine rack. No luck there, either.

A noise at one of the windows made her whip around, heart pounding, but she could see nothing. When she'd entered the room, she hadn't noticed the outside shutters were closed, a fact that gave her the creeps.

Without a view, the room felt so close, so warm.

The heat of discomfort shot through her and she shifted uneasily. A warning threaded through her consciousness: she'd been stupid to do this without backup. But there'd been no choice. Benno was already wounded. Her fault. If something worse happened to him ...

Realizing her imagination was starting to work overtime, that she was conjuring up danger where there was none, Sydney figured she'd better finish up quickly and get out of the house. Foolish or not, she couldn't wait to leave, to get back to the safety of Benno's Place.

To the safety of Benno's arms, a little voice whispered.

She couldn't think about Benno now or she would lose her motivation and she was almost done.

The only piece of furniture she hadn't yet searched was a storage unit with a half-dozen wide, shallow drawers that would hold architectural drawings or blueprints. Though placing a hanging file in such a unit seemed ridiculous, she couldn't leave without being certain it hadn't been stored there.

The top two drawers held exactly what she'd expected, but she could only pull the third open a few inches. Something wedged inside was jamming it, as if Kenneth had hastily shoved in the contents. Because he didn't want someone else to see him put it there? She squeezed her fingers through the opening and tried to work the papers loose while pulling on the handle. The drawer gave and flew open into her stomach.

And in the middle of the drawer sat a red file tagged Lord, Martha.

With a sense of elation, she opened it. Inside were three matching red folders marked Estate, Personal, and School.

The Estate folder held the documents that granted Kenneth total power over the distribution of Martha's trust until she was twenty-five unless he gave up or was, for some reason, unable to fulfill said duty. Or unless she married with his consent. If Martha married without his consent, however, Kenneth would then have power over her trust for an additional five years.

Martha was presently twenty-three, Sydney thought. And a dead man would have an impossible time overseeing a trust.

Another noise made Sydney jump and a jolt of fear surge straight to her chest, which immediately tightened. She listened but couldn't identify the source. It was the wind, she reminded herself uneasily, hurrying to open the Personal folder with trembling fingers.

As she did, the breath caught in her throat. A stack of correspondence was topped by a copy of a letter addressed to one Alan Foxglove.

Alan Foxglove . . . Al Fox. Obviously the same man using an alias!

Eagerly, Sydney read the letter:

Mr. Alan Foxglove:

After having a long, heartfelt talk with my sister, I understand she wants to marry you. While I sympathized with Martha's wish to have a family of her own, I found your whirlwind courtship and failure to open your background to scrutiny suspect.

Therefore, I did some checking on my own through a discreet private detective. He found that Alan Foxglove does not exist and followed you until he unearthed your true identity. I know you to be one Albert Fox, that you have served time in prison for theft—stealing jewels from two other wealthy young women, to be precise.

I do not want to hurt Martha with the truth. If you pursue my sister and she continues her relationship with you, I will be forced to cut off her funds immediately. If you somehow marry without my knowledge, she will not come into any money until she is thirty. I do not think a man such as yourself would be satisfied with this arrangement.

If you have even the slightest feeling for Martha, you will make whatever excuses you need to end this travesty and leave her in peace ... and in ignorance of your true intentions.

Respectfully,
Kenneth Lord

"Al Fox, a fortune hunter and a jewel thief!" Sydney murmured, things now coming together and starting to make sense to her.

Of course Martha had known Al Fox. But she had known him as Alan Foxglove. Martha was a rich young woman, the perfect prey for a good-looking and charming if unscrupulous man—the same villain who had seduced Sydney into believing she was so loved.

Sydney was now certain she should find out why the newspaper clipping had been in Fox's room. The man would have to have some grudge against her, some reason to hate her enough to set her up for murder. What in the world could that reason be?

And what about Martha Lord? Had the young woman plotted her brother's murder with Alan Foxglove? Had she been willing to involve an innocent woman for her own financial gain? Or to be with the man she loved?

Sydney took a deep breath ... and was suddenly sickened by the very real smell of smoke. She sniffed the air. Something burning nearby. Looking around, she saw a thick stream of gray curl through the crack beneath the study door.

Fire!

The house was on fire! And she wasn't naive enough to think this was any accident.

The noises she'd heard *had* been made by a human being—one who obviously wanted her dead! She'd been too caught up in her find to pay heed to the warning. Folding the copy of the letter, Sydney stuffed it into her skirt pocket alongside the tarot deck and ran to the study door.

Locked!

Trying not to panic, she kicked the wooden panel but to no avail. That exit probably wouldn't be safe, anyway, she told herself. She could feel the heat and hear the crackle of burning wood through the door. The smoke coming through the crack was even heavier now. Covering her nose and mouth with her hands, Sydney looked to the windows. The shutters were heavy and secured from the outside.

Wondering what she could use to break through one of them, she moved away from the door.

A split second later, the room went black.

"*Sydney....*"

Her heartbeat went wild at the familiar whisper and she turned toward the sound before she had time to think about what she was doing. Fox must be in the room with her, she realized, as she bumped into the edge of the wall unit. In the dark, she had no way of knowing exactly where, but he sounded close.

A thrill of fear shot down her spine as she thought about being alone with him.

"*Sydney, my love....*"

Him and his gun.

She held her breath to see if she could pinpoint Fox's whereabouts. The only thing she heard was a soft hiss. The fire? Surely not. But what else could it be? Taking a shallow breath, she drew in some smoke and forced herself to hold back a cough. Her mind twirled as she tried to guess how Fox had gotten into the room. She hadn't noticed another door, but if he'd gotten in, she could get out, she told herself encouragingly. All she had to do was avoid him and find the exit in the dark.

"Sydney, my love, I'm waiting. Come to me."

The hope of escape died as Sydney realized the sound was as much acoustic as human. Fox wasn't there at all. The hiss was coming from the speakers in the wall unit. His voice was being piped in from somewhere else.

This is how he had done it, then, frightening her to the edge of despair. He'd recorded his voice, used some kind of amplification system to play the same words and phrases over and over in the same eerie way.

And she was certain he was doing so now merely because he enjoyed her fear.

Another sound—the crackle and pop of burning wood—made her turn to see flames licking the edges of the door. The fire was spreading fast, no doubt because of the amount of timber in the house and aided by the high wind.

Dear God, unless she found a way out fast, she would be trapped in a raging inferno!

Chapter Thirteen

Benno saw the flames long before he was halfway to the Lord house. He only hoped someone else in town had been as observant and had called the fire department. The high winds would fuel the fire that would then spread wildly. He drove as fast as he dared up the winding road.

A torch against the midnight sky, the house on the cliff lit his way.

Praying that Sydney wasn't inside, Benno cursed himself bitterly for having let her out of his sight. He should have known she would do something desperate. She'd acted so odd after they'd made love that he shouldn't have trusted her to have the good sense to stay put.

The next second Benno was castigating himself for trying to make Sydney into some child who needed to be told what to do. She was a woman.

The woman he loved.

He'd only loved twice in his life. Nissa had been dead for twenty years. Sydney couldn't die, too.

If she did, he'd have another death on his conscience. He shouldn't have encouraged her to go looking for trouble. He should have insisted on hiring a private detective instead of tearing around the countryside with her. He was a jinx, no good to any woman. That's why he'd never looked for love. Sydney had just happened to him.

Let her live, he prayed fiercely. *Let Sydney be somewhere safe.*

He hadn't been able to save Nissa, but he'd be damned if he'd watch Sydney die. He'd save her somehow. And if she never wanted to be near him again afterward, he wouldn't fight her. He would be content that she was alive.

He hadn't asked for much on this earth. Surely he was due one favor.

But as he pulled up the driveway, Benno spotted Sydney's car and he knew she was still inside. He didn't see how she could survive when the entire house seemed to be wreathed in flames. He couldn't give up. Wouldn't! He would find her and bring her to safety if it was the last thing he ever did!

Benno jumped out of the car and wavered for a second, unsure which direction to take until he heard Sydney's screams.

TRAPPED BY THE DARK, a blackness deeper than any she had ever experienced before, Sydney knew her vision was coming true.

She was suffocating…couldn't breathe…couldn't scream for help again.

No one to hear.

No exit.

Choking on the smoke that was filling the room, she tried a window but couldn't free the lock. The glass. She could break the glass.

Find something heavy, she told herself, going over the room in her mind.

The speakers.

Heat seared her as she stumbled to the wall unit and blindly searched the top shelf. The fire roared to her left. She could barely see the flames through the thick smoke that made her eyes burn and tear. Her fingers found the front panel of a speaker. She grasped it with both hands and pulled, but wires prevented her from pulling it free.

She jerked hard—once, twice, three times. Finally, the speaker came free, the momentum carrying her several steps across the room. She stumbled, and, unable to catch herself, went flying headfirst. Stars lit the blackness and she dropped the speaker. Her hand grasped a ledge. She'd run into the drawing table.

No time to wait for the pain to recede, she told herself as she started coughing.

Picking up the speaker and using the drawing table as a guide, she worked her way around to the window farthest from the fire. Then she backed off, closed her eyes to protect them, and swung her arms in a broad arc.

She let the speaker fly and continued turning. With her back to the window, she covered her face as glass shattered and sprayed her. A sharp pain in the back of her neck made her wince. She freed the jagged piece of glass and advanced to the window, her foot brushing the speaker where it had fallen to the floor. Aware of the razor-sharp edges that would be left along the pane, she carefully felt for the shutters, then shoved at the wooden barrier with all her might.

It didn't budge.

Don't panic. Just figure a way to get through, she told herself.

Her lungs felt as if they'd been seared and were on the verge of collapse, her head ached and her neck stung, yet Sydney found the strength somewhere. She felt for the speaker with her foot, hoping it would be heavy enough to pop the locks if she banged it against the shutters.

"Sydney!"

Her name came from outside. She froze until she realized it wasn't Fox who was calling her name.

"Benno!" She croaked out his name and turned back to the shutters. She slammed both palms into the wood.

"Sydney? Where are you?"

She hit the shutters again, this time with her fists. "Here!" The word was swallowed as she began choking on the smoke.

"Hold on!"

The clack of bolts being released was a welcome sound. A harsh cough racked her slender body. The shutters opened and, caught by the wind, whipped back against the side of the building. The air she gulped made her cough even harder. Her eyes watered so much she could hardly see.

"Come on, but be careful of the glass," Benno warned.

She blinked to clear her eyes. *His arms were stretched out, reaching for her....* Just as they had been in the vision! Sydney thought.

"Get away!" she yelled, trying to climb out herself. His life was in danger if he stayed. Her skirt caught on a giant shard, sending her off balance. Her

left hand shot out and nicked a spiked piece of glass.
"A-a-h!"

"Let me help you," Benno said grimly, placing his
hands around her waist as she righted herself on the
sill.

"No!" she croaked. "I can do it. Get away from
here now!"

But Benno ignored her and pulled her free of certain death.

Sydney's mind whirled. This wasn't supposed to be
happening. She had tried to take charge, to turn her
back on the man she loved so she could save him. But
the vision was coming true anyway.

Benno led her a safe distance from the burning
house to the nearby stand of trees. Despite the wind
that tore at her skirt, Sydney couldn't seem to get her
breath. She tried to control the cough but felt as if she
were choking.

"Let's stop here," Benno said, forcing her to sit on
a fallen tree not far from where she'd found Kenneth
Lord's body. "Try to take deep breaths."

What she tried was to tell him to get away while he
could, but she couldn't find her voice to warn him. His
full attention was centered on her and she knew the
warning would be futile. He wouldn't leave her.

And then it was too late.

From the corner of her eye, she glimpsed movement. She turned as a dark figure bore down on them,
arms swinging. Though her eyes were still tearing, she
saw the board as it struck Benno's wounded arm.

"Aagh!" Clutching it, Benno sank to his knees.

"No, stop!" she screamed hoarsely, pushing herself up from the log.

Another hit across the back of his head had Benno sprawled across the ground. He lay still, apparently unconscious.

Sydney jumped on his assailant only to be thrown to the side as the man pulled out a gun...the same gun she'd seen in her dream. He poked Benno with his toe. When he got no response, he turned the gun on her.

And Sydney had no doubts she was looking at a murderer.

His lips turned up in a crooked smile. "Sydney, my love."

She was facing the man she thought she'd married...the man who more recently had wanted to marry Martha.

"Al Fox," she said when she regained her breath. "Or should I call you Alan Foxglove?" she asked.

"Or maybe you would prefer Alexander Foxworth, the name your old friend Candace knew me by," he returned with that crooked grin that had once won her heart.

Sydney's jaw dropped. Fox. Foxglove. Foxworth.

"Of course," she whispered, dazed. "I knew I should have been able to figure it out. I found the newspaper clipping you left in your apartment. I knew whoever was trying to frame me had to be someone from my past." Though she had never met her friend's fiancé, and therefore wouldn't have recognized him. "And I found a letter from the real Kenneth Lord to you, mentioning some rich women whose jewels you'd stolen—one of whom must have been Candace," she said, remembering her friend's sad tale. "If only I had remembered the name Lex Foxworth sooner—"

Fox laughed. "Too bad you didn't use those psychic abilities of yours to figure out who I was when you met me."

Though she hadn't used those abilities in years, had, in fact, suppressed them, they had started kicking in, trying to warn her of danger even before she met her "Kenneth." She'd been too burned-out, too willing to believe she was going crazy to interpret what was happening to her.

"You might have been able to get away," Fox went on. "I would have followed you, of course. I've been dreaming of this moment for almost four years."

"How could anyone be so obsessed?"

"You took away my meal ticket."

Wondering if she could keep him talking until help came—surely someone had reported the fire—she said, "And you found another wealthy woman. Martha."

"Only after doing time because of you. Candy told me you warned her about me when she had me arrested for stealing her jewelry."

"And you wanted to frame me for that?"

"Hey, one good turn deserves another."

With his free hand, Fox grabbed Sydney's wrist and dragged her along the path through the trees.

"What are you doing?" she demanded, her heart wildly pounding. The man was a killer, capable of anything. "Where are you taking me?"

She glanced back at Benno who hadn't moved and prayed he would be all right. And then she looked at the house. He'd gotten her out just in time. It was starting to collapse. Soon nothing would be left standing.

"When I clipped that article about you out of the newspaper," Fox said, "I knew I would find a way to get to you. I took it out and looked at it every day I was in stir. I never guessed how easy it would be to track you down and win your trust. Then, when you fell in love with me, I was positive I could take care of both Lord and you in one neat plan."

"Your plan isn't so neat anymore."

"That's why I have to tidy things up."

"The way you did with the photographs?" she asked.

"That was pretty clever of me, I have to admit. I knew you couldn't go flashing those pictures around or Martha would recognize me. You made things easy by leaving the camera where you dropped it until the next day. I switched the film before you went back for it. Worked right into my master plan. Now everyone will think you committed suicide because you had a breakdown. They'll be convinced you killed Kenneth Lord."

Suicide. How close she'd come the day she stumbled over Kenneth Lord's body. But if she'd survived that episode, she would survive this, Sydney vowed. She needed to keep him talking until she could figure out how.

"Did you plan Kenneth's murder alone or was Martha the brains behind the operation?"

Fox laughed. "That idiot? She doesn't know anything. Even if she does have suspicions, she'll keep her mouth shut. She's as gullible as you were—she thinks I love her and can't wait to marry me. No, this brilliant plan is all mine."

So neither Martha nor anyone else had been involved in Kenneth's death, after all. "What are you planning to do to me?" she asked, although she knew he was taking her to the cliff, the site of his "accident."

"Since you wouldn't break and throw yourself off as I had hoped, and since you didn't stay put in the fire, I'll have to give you some help. Your body will probably wash up on the beach with the morning's tide. I haven't figured out what I'll do with De-Martino's body."

Benno? Sydney felt as if she'd been struck. "You can't kill him."

"Watch me." He laughed. "Oops—I almost forgot you won't be able to."

"But Benno didn't do anything to you." She was getting panicky now that reality was setting in. Not only was she in mortal danger, but so was the man she loved! "You have no score to settle with him."

"He got in my way."

They'd cleared the trees and were approaching the area where she'd stood to take pictures of her "new husband." The wind whipped at them, pushing them forward.

Trying to think of a way to escape his plan, she stalled by asking, "How did you fake your death?"

"There's a ledge just below where I 'slipped.' I had enough time to duck behind an overhang, so you couldn't see me from the water. A risky performance, I admit, but well worth the reward."

Hoping to catch Fox off guard, Sydney purposely stumbled over one of the fissures in the rock. Though she went down to her knees, Fox continued on, dragging her. Desperate, she started screaming.

"Help! Anyone! Murderer!"

"Shut up!"

Stopping long enough to pull her to her feet, he tried to cover her mouth with his gun hand. Sydney bit down and elbowed him. He lost his grip both on her and on the weapon. The gun went skittering off into the dark.

She made her break back the way they'd come, her chest heaving with the effort as she ran against the wind. The smoke had wreaked havoc with her lungs and her strength was draining away with every step. Fox followed and, in two seconds, had her by the arm. The cough started again and she gave up for the moment. At least he hadn't gone after the gun. Now he wouldn't be able to find the weapon while still keeping hold of her.

"We can do this easy or rough," he said, jerking her around. "You choose."

Gasping for air, she said, "I'll take rough!"

Sydney struggled, kicking and pummeling him with the little strength she had left, but this time she lost her footing. She went down hard. Rather than righting her, Fox merely grabbed her by the ankle and dragged her toward the precipice. Her skirt rode up to her thighs and her free leg took a beating against the stone. Ignoring the pain, she tried kicking Fox with her loose foot, but he was ready for the attempted strike and danced out of her way.

They were getting close to the edge of the cliff.

Too close.

Sydney changed tactics. She clawed at the ground, trying to find a hold. Her fingers scraped raw across the rocky surface. Winded, she tried to catch her breath. Finally, with a burst of strength that could only come from adrenaline manufactured by desperation, she reached out and caught hold of a boulder with both arms. She brought Fox to a sudden halt that jarred her bones and made her teeth clack together.

"Son-of-a—"

"Get away from her!" came a nearby shout.

Benno. Moonlight haloed her dark knight who came charging after them. He was all right then. And Fox no longer had the gun. Benno wouldn't die, after all. Maybe they would both come out of this alive.

Fox grabbed a handful of Sydney's hair and jerked hard, making her let go of the rock. "Come closer and I'll kill her," he warned Benno.

She found the strength to shout, "He doesn't have the gun any more and he intends to kill me anyway!"

"A gun wouldn't stop me," Benno said, still bearing down on them.

As he drew closer and she could see him more clearly, Sydney realized he wasn't in the best of shape. He was holding his bad arm stiffly and he looked drawn as if he were in a great deal of pain. She could tell Fox was uncertain about his strategy, but she doubted he would run and forfeit his entire scheme.

She felt like a puppet as, still holding on to her hair, Fox whipped her forward in Benno's path. She crashed into him while Fox scrambled and tried to find the gun.

"You all right?" Benno asked.

"Yes."

Like a shot, he took off after Fox who was bending over, arm outstretched. Fear gripped Sydney for a moment, but Benno got to Fox before Fox could pick up the gun. He kicked the murderer square in the stomach. Bent over, Fox rushed him and knocked Benno off balance so he stumbled closer toward the edge of the cliff.

Sydney realized Benno was still dazed and vulnerable. In his condition, he was no match for the other man. She had to get to him, to help him before it was too late! She couldn't lose him now!

She rushed forward, but Benno yelled, "Stay out of the way!"

Though she did as he ordered, she looked around for a makeshift weapon while the two men traded punches. Benno held his own until Fox rushed him again and with both fists closed hit him in the wounded arm. Benno whirled away from him, closer to the cliff's edge. No weapon.

This was all her fault!

Desperate, Sydney acted on instinct—she grabbed the tarot deck in her pocket!

Sliding it out, she shrieked, "Fox!" as she threw the pouch.

The deck caught him square in the chest, startling him. The cards flew up and out of the opening and the wind tossed them in every direction. Sydney's ploy worked. He hesitated long enough for Benno to get in one more punch, making Fox take a step backward.

His face a mask of surprise, Fox did a macabre dance and lost his balance. His feet went out from under him.

"Help me!" he yelled as his lower body shot over the side. He threw his chest forward and tried to grasp the smooth rock. He began to slide backward.

Without thinking, Sydney ran toward him and grabbed his wrist, unwilling to let another human being die, not even one as rotten as Fox. Her mistake. In the blink of an eye, his fingers curled around her wrist.

"No!" Sydney cried, even as she fought for release. "Let go!"

But she was no match for a madman—her body shot forward.

The only thing that saved her was Benno grabbing onto her long skirt. Her view was dizzying. She could see the breakers crash against the wall of the rock and spew a shattered curtain of water up at them.

"If I go, you go!" Fox yelled.

With his greater weight dragging at her, she could do nothing to save herself.

"Like hell!" Benno growled. Pinning her skirt to the ground with his knee, he got down beside her and anchored an arm around her waist. "Pull yourself up, Fox. You aren't taking anyone else with you."

Their position was precarious. Sydney knew they could all go over. Fox made a futile attempt to raise himself, but his exhaustion was apparent as his grip began to slip.

"Try harder," she urged, even as his fingers slid over hers.

"No-o-o!"

Fox was falling, no ledge to save him this time.

His body bounced off the cliff face and like a broken doll flew into the mouth of a giant wave. Before it could toss him back to batter him against the cliff, she buried her head in Benno's chest. He pulled her close and held her for a moment.

"Could anyone survive a fall like that?" she asked, deep shudders wracking her body.

"No."

Closing her eyes, she fought back the tears. For a short while, she'd cared for this man, this villain, no matter how misguidedly. She would never forget that, or him. His death would remain imprinted in her mind always.

"Let's get out of here."

As Benno helped her to her feet, Sydney noticed a single tarot card wedged in a crack near the edge. The others had undoubtedly been sucked up by the ocean just as Fox had been. Sydney picked up the card and a chill swept through her as she stared at the picture: a woman holding a sword in one hand, scales in the other.

How could she not recognize Justice when she saw it?

THE LAST FIRE TRUCK pulled away from the shell of a once-beautiful house. Martha leaned against the police car, sobbing and stroking the leather jacket that had belonged to Al Fox.

"I don't believe it," Martha cried as Brickman called in his report. "He killed my brother and then made love to me as if I were the only woman in the world." Her eyes met Sydney's for a second, then flicked away.

Brickman had told them that Fox had a checkered criminal record. His specialty had been duping wealthy women, and until a few months ago, his home had been a prison in Washington State.

"I think my car is an insurance write-off," Sydney said, shaking her head. Flaming timbers had fallen on it, denting the hood and roof, setting fire to the upholstery. "You're lucky your Thunderbird's okay."

"I wouldn't have cared, as long as you were all right."

Their eyes met and Sydney realized how much she loved Benno. Before she could tell him, Brickman approached them.

"I'm heading back to town." The policeman looked at Sydney, his expression devoid of his usual belligerence. "Where will I find you tomorrow?"

"My place," Benno said. "Right?"

"His place," Sydney agreed.

Brickman nodded and returned to his vehicle. He helped Martha into the passenger seat where she sat as if she were in shock. He started the engine and backed down the driveway.

"I actually feel sorry for her," Sydney said, following Benno to the Thunderbird. "She really loved him."

"What about you?" he asked tersely.

"I thought I did, but I was mistaken." She sensed he was waiting for more. "I wasn't mistaken about you though. I love you and want to be with you."

Benno stopped and stared down at her intently. "With me? What exactly does that mean?"

"It means I don't want to rush into anything this time."

"Why? Because of my past?"

Sydney glanced out over the property toward the cliff. It would be tough staying in Stone Beach with that constant reminder of her folly and of the terror she'd been through always in sight. But being with the man she loved would help her forget.

"I don't care about your past, Benno. I care about the human being you are. I told you that before. I just want to take things slow," she explained, "make sure we both know how we feel." She tried to lighten the heavy atmosphere. "So, if I'm going to stay for a while, I'll need a job. You could hire me to read tarot cards at Benno's Place."

"You're kidding, right?" When she shook her head, Benno said, "You can't really have so much faith in those things."

"I don't live by them, if that's what you mean. I think of them as a kind of tool to help people feel good. I need something to make *me* feel better— maybe I've relied on them too heavily recently," she admitted. "But things are clearer now. I know I have to trust in myself."

"And in your psychic powers?"

"I hope they won't get in the way. I want to be like other people, Benno. I always have. I don't want to feel different or be afraid anymore." She placed her hand on his chest, over his heart. "With you, I think I can handle anything."

"I want that inner peace for you, Sydney." He frowned. "But what about your advertising career? I can't ask you to give that up."

"I never meant to go back to it. I was looking for peace and quiet, a change of life-style."

"Instead, you found Al Fox."

"And then I found you. Give us some time to know each other better," she pleaded, running her hand up to his stubbled cheek and putting her fingers under a loose strand of hair at his temple. "We might decide we have a future together . . . if that's good enough for you."

"Enough?" Benno pulled her to his chest and wound his arms around her. "That's better than I hoped for. I thought you would leave town and never look back. I love you, Sydney Raferty, and I don't ever intend to let you go.''

Sydney gave him a brilliant smile as he bent to kiss her. Not every woman had her own dark knight.

Epilogue

The room felt small and dank, the tension-riddled atmosphere cloying. King Crawley bunched up the newspaper Lester Freidman had given him and slammed it on the table. The walls of his prison had never seemed so confining.

"Damn! If I could get out, I'd do the job right! I shoulda known Fox was too good to be true."

His fellow convict had been a man not only ready, but eager to do his dirty work.

Freidman paled and kept his voice low. "What do we do now? Are you going to find another way to get to the woman."

Glancing toward the guard at the door who was paid well to ignore his business, Crawley shook his head. "I'm done with her."

"That's it, then?"

Crawley thought Freidman looked relieved. Must be getting soft without the right man on his tail. Crawley wondered how badly his organization was crumbling. He couldn't do everything from a prison cell.

"Don't be stupid," he finally told the erstwhile accountant. "Dakota Raferty is gonna be our next target."

Harlequin Intrigue®

QUID PRO QUO

Vengeance Is Mine.... Sydney Raferty narrowly escaped King Crawley's wrath in PUSHED TO THE LIMIT. Pursued by a man bent on revenge, she triumphed over evil and found her way back to reality with the love of Benno DeMartino.

Revenge Is Sweet.... Driven by an insatiable need to ruin the Raferty family, King Crawley strikes again next month in #163 SQUARING ACCOUNTS (June 1991). Dakota Raferty is a man whose honest nature falls prey to Crawley's madness. Sydney's brother is an unsuspecting pawn in a game of deadly revenge.

An Eye For An Eye.... Asia, the youngest of the Raferty siblings, is next, in #165 NO HOLDS BARRED, the final chapter in the QUID PRO QUO series (July 1991). Stalked by King Crawley—a man now insane with the desire to kill—she must find a way to end the vendetta. And only one man can help—Dominic Crawley. But will the racketeer's son join forces with Asia to end his father's quest for revenge?

Don't miss the next two books in Patricia Rosemoor's QUID PRO QUO trilogy coming to you from Harlequin Intrigue.

QPQ

Back by Popular Demand

Janet Dailey
Americana

A romantic tour of America through fifty favorite Harlequin Presents® novels, each set in a different state researched by Janet and her husband, Bill. A journey of a lifetime in one cherished collection.

In June, don't miss the sultry states featured in:

Title # 9 - **FLORIDA**
       Southern Nights
   #10 - **GEORGIA**
       Night of the Cotillion

Available wherever
Harlequin books are sold.

You'll flip . . . your pages won't!
Read paperbacks *hands-free* with

Book Mate • I

The perfect "mate" for all your romance paperbacks

Traveling • Vacationing • At Work • In Bed • Studying • Cooking • Eating

Perfect size for all standard paperbacks, this wonderful invention makes reading a pure pleasure! Ingenious design holds paperback books OPEN and FLAT so even wind can't ruffle pages — leaves your hands free to do other things. Reinforced, wipe-clean vinyl-covered holder flexes to let you turn pages without undoing the strap . . . supports paperbacks so well, they have the strength of hardcovers!

Pages turn WITHOUT opening the strap

SEE-THROUGH STRAP

Reinforced back stays flat

Built in bookmark

BOOK MARK

BACK COVER HOLDING STRIP

10" x 7¼", opened
Snaps closed for easy carrying, too

Available now. Send your name, address, and zip code, along with a check or money order for just $5.95 + 75¢ for delivery (for a total of $6.70) payable to Reader Service to:

Reader Service
Bookmate Offer
3010 Walden Avenue
P.O. Box 1396
Buffalo, N.Y. 14269-1396

Offer not available in Canada
*New York residents add appropriate sales tax.

BM-GR